Scandalous Engagement with a Governess

HISTORICAL REGENCY ROMANCE NOVEL

Dorothy Sheldon

Copyright © 2021 by Dorothy Sheldon
All Rights Reserved.
This book may not be reproduced or transmitted in any form without the written permission of the publisher. In no way is it legal to reproduce, duplicate, or transmit any part of this document in either electronic means or in printed format. Recording of this publication is strictly prohibited and any storage of this document is not allowed unless with written permission from the publisher.

Table of Contents

Prologue..3
Chapter One...8
Chapter Two 16
Chapter Three..24
Chapter Four..31
Chapter Five...38
Chapter Six...45
Chapter Seven..52
Chapter Eight...59
Chapter Nine..63
Chapter Ten 67
Chapter Eleven...71
Chapter Twelve..75
Chapter Thirteen..80
Chapter Fourteen 87
Chapter Fifteen..94
Chapter Sixteen 101
Chapter Seventeen 108
Chapter Eighteen 116
Chapter Nineteen 120
Chapter Twenty 127
Chapter Twenty-One 132
Chapter Twenty-Two 136
Chapter Twenty-Three...141
Chapter Twenty-Four...148
Chapter Twenty-Five..152
Chapter Twenty-Six..157
Chapter Twenty-Seven 163
Chapter Twenty-Eight..167
Chapter Twenty-Nine...172
Chapter Thirty..176
Epilogue 180

Prologue

Many Years Ago

It was a fine day for a picnic. Perfect, in fact.

Plenty of families had the same idea, setting up picnic blankets wherever they could, politely but firmly eyeing other families who dared to edge too close. Everyone wanted a nice view of the lake, of course, but not too close as to tempt the ducks from the water or find themselves on boggy ground. The prime spots were under the trees, which provided plenty of cool shade in the hot summer sun, and an unparalleled view of the scenery before them.

If the details of the outing had been left to Mrs Barlow, they likely wouldn't have found themselves a spot at all, let alone such a prime position.

Mrs Darnell, thankfully, had come out here early in the morning, before anyone else could tell that the day would be a fine one, and left her unfortunate maid in charge of guarding the spot. The sun was now high in the sky, and a steady heat filtered down to the people below.

"What a perfect day." Mrs Barlow remarked, leaning back on her elbows. Mrs Darnell sat bolt upright, neck craned to watch their respective children.

"I do hope that Ewan and Hope don't go near to the water." Mrs Darnell said anxiously. "I made Ewan promise that he wouldn't before we left. He can swim, but that's really not the point."

"If that boy of yours promised to steer clear of the water, he'll do so." Mrs Barlow said lazily. "You ought to give him more credit. Show a little more trust, Margaret, my dear. You worry entirely too much. The children will be fine."

Mrs Darnell snorted, watching the two distant specks take a turn towards the clump of trees nearby. One of them – Ewan, she thought – stayed where he was, burying his hands in his face, while the other darted off towards the trees. She could almost hear the counting.

"They're playing hide and seek." She murmured. "I hope they don't play too well. I don't fancy one of them getting lost."

Mrs Barlow squinted against the sun, watching the children. "Hope and Ewan are six and eight years old respectively, and Ewan is a very sensible little boy. We've been here before, and they've always behaved well. Ewan won't let Hope get into trouble, and she rarely lets him out of her sight. They'll be quite alright so long as they stay together. I've said it before, Margaret, and I'll say it again. You worry entirely too much."

Mrs Darnell seemed to relax a little, but not nearly enough.

"If I worry too much, Emmeline, you don't worry enough. I hate to say it, but sometimes it's better to anticipate disasters. Then you'll never be disappointed."

Mrs Barlow chuckled. "Good things come to those who wait, Margaret."

Mrs Darnell was not listening anymore. She watched Hope disappear into the woods entirely, and nibbled on her lip nervously.

"Not always, I'm afraid. In fact, I'd say that patient people are seldom, if ever rewarded. I wish you wouldn't be so trusting, Emmeline. Hope follows your example."

"And that's a bad thing? To be too trusting?"

There was a brief pause.

"Yes." Mrs Darnell said eventually. "Yes, I'm afraid it is."

Ewan could almost feel his mother's anxious, watchful eyes on him. He kept his hands over his eyes and continued diligently counting. They'd agreed he would count to fifty, and now he wished he'd chosen a nearer number. The clatter of Hope's stiff-soled shoes had long since faded away, but he'd heard the tell-tale rustle of dry leaves and foliage, so he knew she'd gone into the woods.

Not too far, he hoped.

"Forty-eight, forty-nine, fifty!" Ewan chanted. "Ready or not, here I come!"

He heard a vague call from his mother, something about being careful, and paused to smile and wave up the hill. He sometimes wished that his mamma would be a little bit more like Hope's mamma, who was always relaxed and calm, and always let Hope do more or less what she liked. Ewan's mamma was a little more nervous, always clinging onto Ewan's hand in public and lifting him up into carriages when he could easily climb in himself.

He was eight years old, for heaven's sake.

Ewan ran into the forest, ducking under low-hanging branches and stepping over gnarled roots. It was much cooler here, under the trees, and it smelt fresh too – of wet grass and deliciously damp earth. He hoped that Hope wouldn't have chosen anywhere muddy for her hiding place. Her dress today was pastel-pink and would stain easily.

Hope's mamma would probably just laugh and give the dress to the laundress, but Ewan's mamma would squawk and lecture.

A few steps into the forest, and Ewan stopped to look around.

There was an art to hide and seek, and he knew it well. You had to think of your opponent, of where they would hide. It was no use trudging doggedly along and searching every hiding place.

For example, when he played hide and seek with Thomas Potts, he knew that Thomas always panicked and chose the first hiding place he came across. Lucas Mackenzie wouldn't choose anywhere small and tight – like a closet or under a bed – and so on. Elizabeth Martin, who would be a real Lady one day, would never hide anywhere muddy, dirty, or dusty, because it would crumple her clothes.

Hope was a little more difficult to gauge. She could fit into all of the small spaces and wouldn't worry about getting her hair-ribbons caught on branches or her hem stained with mud.

Meaning, unfortunately, that she could be anywhere.

Ewan slowed his pace, head whipping from side to side. Hope was not patient and tended not to take wild risks. Now that meant that she was likely to have picked a hiding spot relatively soon into the woods, instead of barreling on through and risking being caught out without a hiding spot.

A muffled giggle came from somewhere to his left. Ewan swung around that way, eyes narrowing.

There was a large bush with vivid red berries dotted around it. The bright colours would likely have attracted Hope.

He tiptoed towards the bush, holding his breath. The bush shivered a little, and another muffled giggle wafted out from behind.

"Aha!" Ewan crowed, leaping around the bush in one smooth movement. "Got you!"

Hope was curled into a ball at the base of the bush, one hand clapped over her mouth to muffle her giggles. She gave a shriek of shock and delight, falling over onto her backside.

"You're so good at finding, Ewan!" she complained, getting to her feet and shaking out her skirts. "It isn't fair."

"Well, you could be a bit better at hiding if you didn't keep giggling aloud." Ewan pointed out. "I won, by the way."

Hope rolled her eyes. At their respective ages of six and eight, the two children already could not be more different. Ewan had dark hair and chocolate-coloured eyes that were habitually narrowed in suspicion. He was clever, and knew that he was clever, and preferred to think things through carefully before he did anything.

Hope, on the other hand, was a waifish little elf of a child who would one day grow up to be a beautiful woman. She had flaxen coloured curls that were always matted and disarranged, large blue eyes, and pale skin that reddened quickly in the summer sun. Mrs Darnell fretted constantly at that, fearing sunburn or worse – freckles. She'd brought a little parasol today, especially for Hope's use.

The parasol was not, of course, being used.

By a mutual, unspoken decision, the two of them sat down behind the bush, making no move to return to the picnic blanket and their respective mothers.

"Mamma is going to be so upset when she sees how grubby we are." Ewan commented. "We should stay here for a while."

Hope sighed. "My Mamma won't be upset. She's never upset. I sometimes think that she doesn't care very much what I do." She plucked at the hem of her dress, where the pretty lace had been torn a little. "I think I would like Mamma to care a little more, like your mamma does. Your mamma cares about you very much indeed."

Too much, Ewan might have said, but decided against it. He did love his mamma, after all.

"Mammas and papas are strange things, I think." He said absently, and Hope nodded in agreement.

"Very strange. I shouldn't like to be without them, though."

Ewan glanced down at the girl sitting at his side and felt a rush of affection. His papa might say that a man ought to make friends with other men, not girls, but he liked Hope the very best out of everyone else he knew.

"I am glad that we are friends." He said, after a pause.

Hope nodded wisely. "So am I. Exceptionally glad. I hope we'll always be friends."

Ewan considered this. "We should make a promise. A pact that we'll always be friends."

"Yes, I think that's a good idea. How would we go about it?"

Ewan shifted so that he was facing Hope, cross-legged and serious. She coped him.

"You have to repeat after me. I, Ewan Darnell..."

"I, Ewan Darnell..."

"No, use your name in place of mine."

"Oh, of course. Start again."

"I, Ewan Darnell..."

"I, Hope Tabitha Barlow..."

"Do solemnly swear to always be the close friend of you..."

"Do solemnly swear to always be the close friend of you..."

"...Hope Tabitha Barlow."

"...Ewan Darnell."

"Good, now we shake hands. Now it's a bargain, and you and I will always be best friends."

"Always." Hope repeated earnestly.

Chapter One

Present Day

Hope shifted uncomfortably on the hard wooden chairs set out in the waiting room. She'd already been here for a full hour, and might well be here for longer, too.

The employment agency was a familiar place to her now, and she had a feeling that their faces dropped a little further every time they saw her. After all, employment agencies had reputations to uphold, and being connected with a young woman who was so resolutely impossible to place would be a blot on their fine reputation, would it not?

It wasn't Hope's fault, though. Not one bit, although it was getting harder and harder to hold onto that fact as each successive rejection letter came through the post, if a reply came at all. She'd lost track of the jobs she'd applied to.

At the age of twenty-four, with a half-decent Society education behind her, Hope should have found it remarkably easy to find a position as a governess. After all, it wasn't as if she'd be required to teach the children complex mathematics and Latin. No, they only required a light, passing education – dancing, music, art, needlework, English, history, light mathematics, and so on. Hope could do all of those things and prided herself on having a good knack with children and a nice temperament.

And yet, the rejection letters flooded in.

A clerk appeared in the doorway to the waiting room, making Hope flinch. She was now the only one left, the other ladies and gentlemen having gradually gone in and come out, clutching pieces of paper and wearing hopeful expressions on their faces.

"Mr Swill will see you now." The clerk said flatly. He turned on his heel, not bothering to see whether Hope followed him. She scrambled to her feet, collecting her things, and hurried after the disappearing clerk.

"Miss Hope Barlow, is it now?" Mr Swill said, peering at her over his pince-nez. He had a strangely elongated face, like a bloodhound, and a mess of grubby blond hair that was resolutely pulling back from his hairline. Hope hadn't encountered him before on her visits to the employment agency.

"Yes, I am." Hope replied, sitting as straight as she could in the chair opposite the man's desk. They would never recommend a governess who seemed somewhat slovenly or lacking in a certain way, even if it was just something as silly as improper posture.

"And you wish to be a governess?"

"Yes, sir, I do."

Mr Swill pursed his lips, eyeing the paltry, single sheet of paper that encompassed Hope's entire life.

"And you are capable of instructing in Reading, Writing, Arithmetic, History, and the use of the globes, I assume?"

"Yes, very well, and I can also instruct children in dancing, art, creative writing, embroidery, music..."

"Yes, yes." Mr Swill interrupted, waving his hand impatiently. "Your letter here says that you are quite well instructed in accomplishments."

His tone of voice indicated exactly what he thought of accomplishments.

Hope bit her lip, feeling a little silly. "I was under the impression that employers cared about accomplishments."

"Most sensible employers care only about the proper subjects," Mr Swill said severely. "If the household you are engaged to work for only has boys, for instance, such frivolities as music, art, and dancing will not be required. It's customary to engage a dancing-master for young gentlemen."

Hope couldn't quite understand why little boys should be forbidden to engage in music and art, but she wasn't about to argue the fact. Mr Swill seemed to have taken a dislike to her.

So far, Hope seemed to have done business with every other employee of the agency. Apparently, they'd all washed their hands of her, without ever saying what was making her so eminently unemployable.

"As far as I can tell, Miss Barlow, the reason you are finding it so hard to secure a position is due to the lack of references." He glanced up at her, disapproval emanating from his voice. "Can you explain this lack?"

Hope blushed hotly. He was making it sound like it was all somehow her fault, like she was doing something silly which made people not want to hire her.

"I haven't worked as a governess before." Hope said, tilting up her chin. Mr Swill was grating on her nerves, and she was suddenly keen to finish the meeting and get away from him, with whatever crumbs of hope he could throw her way. "What's more, I had never expected that I would have to do so."

Mr Swill tossed her piece of paper onto the desk and leaned back in his chair. He narrowed his eyes, lacing his fingers across his rounded stomach.

"Explain." He said brusquely.

So Hope did.

"I am an only child, and my father was a viscount. He was a good man, and a good father. I am twenty-four now, and when I was twenty-two, I became engaged to a good man. I never assumed I would have to work for my living. After all, I had my father to care for me, and a fine fiancé, and my own dowry. I was quite comfortable."

"Go on." Mr Swill said, with the tiniest hint of interest in his voice.

Hope drew in a breath. The next part was never easy to explain, no matter how quickly she trotted out the plain, painful facts.

"It transpired that my father had been making bad investments. Playing cards, gambling, I'm sure you can imagine. His debts caught up with him abruptly, and he was taken to debtor's prison. He remains there today. I visit him occasionally, but I have no way of freeing him. None of us can. And then, when my fiancé found out the truth, he immediately broke off the engagement."

"What a cad." Mr Swill murmured, and Hope felt a flare of affection towards him. She could still remember the expression of shock and disgust in Auric's face, when she'd laid out the whole, sordid story before him. It seemed strange to think that she'd hoped he would be able to help out her father. It had never really crossed her mind that he would not want to help. She'd been calculating what Auric could do to make the Viscount more comfortable, when all along Auric was thinking of how quickly he could disentangle himself from the engagement.

Very quickly and efficiently, as it turned out. Hope was too shocked to kick up a fuss about being jilted or do anything petty like try and tear Auric's reputation to shreds.

She wasn't sure she would have wanted to do that, anyway. Besides, they immediately began to move in very different circles. Auric's position in Society was unchanged – he was still Lord Pembroke, a great catch that had just become available again – whereas Hope's would never be the same.

She hadn't run into him since their last, awkward meeting, and that was probably for the best.

Hope shifted her position on the hard chair, clearing her throat and hoping the conversation would move along.

"So, you see, I have no fiancé, no father to care for me, and no money of my own. I was to have had a dowry, of course, but naturally that was eaten up in payment of Papa's debts. There's nothing left now, and the debts still remain."

"What about your mother?"

Something clenched inside Hope. The porridge her aunt had insisted she eat that morning for breakfast bubbled warningly inside her.

"My mother died when I was eighteen years old." Hope said softly. "Her death was what sent my Papa spiraling into debt, gambling, and bad living, I'm afraid."

Mr Swill looked away. "Well, I'm sorry for that. I hate to be blunt, Miss Barlow, but tales of your tragic life will not help you secure a position."

"I know that!" Hope said, stung.

"I only mean to say that you have a good reason for not having references, but this is not a reason that will resonate with your prospective employers. Nobody likes to think of how quickly bad luck and tragedy may catch up with a person. A good governess must be like a good piece of furniture. A chair, perhaps. Functional, reliable, and always there when you need it, but not in a way that catches the eye or distracts the attention. Do you understand?"

"I do, sir."

Mr Swill gave a short nod, drumming his fingers on the desk. He eyed her for a moment or two, chewing his lip.

"It would be better if you were plainer." He murmured.

"Excuse me?"

"I am not, of course, implying that you would allow yourself to sully your reputation in any way. However, you are a very pretty young woman, and I daresay some ladies might feel uncomfortable with having you in their home, alongside their husbands and sons. I do not mean to be offensive, Miss Barlow, but these uncomfortable facts must be addressed."

Hope was sure she had gone beet red. She knew this already, unfortunately. One of her applications had been accepted, and she had gone to meet the lady of the house. The woman's face had dropped when she saw Hope, and her husband's face had lit up.

He had spent the rest of the interview being odiously courteous, and staring at her face for far too long, while the lady of the house made sour compliments on Hope's beauty, remarks which sounded like insults more than anything else. She'd known then that she wouldn't get the job and had a nasty suspicion that the woman had written into the agency to complain about her for some reason.

Hope knew, in a disinterested sort of way, that she was beautiful. She had smooth flaxen curls, pulled back in a neat, demure knot. Her face was oval and well-featured, with a pair of large blue eyes and a bow-shaped mouth. In short, she'd grown up to look almost exactly like her mother, whose picture still hung in her aunt's hallway.

But looks meant very little. Mrs Barlow had made that clear when Hope was growing up. Prettiness faded, and handsomeness could conceal all sorts of character flaws. Hope had always concentrated on improving her mind, and becoming the sort of person her mother would have approved of.

And yet here she was, being reduced to her face and her ability with the use of globes. Were ladies really judging her on whether or not she was likely to tempt their husbands to distraction, and not listening at all to anything else?

"That is not fair." Hope said. "I would rather my employers think about my accomplishments and abilities."

"Yes, that would be sensible, wouldn't it? But the plain fact is that they won't. Combined with your lack of references, that puts us in an uncomfortable position."

Hope sank back into the seat, giving up on her ramrod-straight posture. There wasn't much point anymore, was there?

"Go on, then." She said tiredly. "Tell me that you don't have any positions for me. I'm quite used to rejection by now, and I can accept it with grace."

Mr Swill eyed her for a long moment.

"Actually," he said, his voice slow and hesitant. "I think perhaps I might have something."

***

Mrs Ruth Havisham, widowed, lived in a house in Salisbury Crescent. It had once been a very fine and fashionable area but had certainly seen better days.

It was easy to tell that Ruth was related to the late Viscountess Helen Barlow. They had the same blonde hair, the same large eyes, the same good-natured good looks that made almost everyone sit up and take a second look. There was barely a full year's age difference between the two. The real difference, however, was that Helen was immortalized forever, cut down at a young age. Her portrait – which Ruth had determinedly saved when the rest of the Barlows' things were sold off, along with their house – hung in the hall, with Helen Barlow frozen in her heyday of beauty and grace.

Ruth, on the other hand, was aging, and not well. Her slim figure was becoming more round as the years went by, her clothes were cheap and practical, and years of constant worrying, scrimping, and scraping had greyed her hair and wrinkled her good-natured face.

Her worry lines were out in force today, as she paced up and down the hall of her once-grand home.

"There you are!" she exclaimed, as Hope let herself in the front door. "You've been gone an age."

"I'm sorry, Aunt Ruth. They kept me waiting for a full hour. You know what the employment agency is like."

Ruth grimaced. "Unfortunately, I do. Come on, you're just in time for luncheon. Agnes is already sitting down. I believe she's pressed some more flowers for you, to put in your scrapbook. You must be exhausted, you poor thing. Was it as awful as last time?"

Hope shook her head. "No, I met with a different man this time, and he was surprisingly helpful. I think I may have a position."

Ruth paused, eyes bulging. "A governess position? Truly?"

"Yes, truly. I don't mean to set myself up for disappointment, but..." Hope hesitated, taking out the little square of paper from her pocket. "I have a good feeling about this placement."

"Well, come on into the dining room, and tell us all about it."

Like the rest of the house, the dining room had seen better days. The once-fine paper was peeling on the walls, with blots of damp and mould covered up by velvet curtains and carefully hung pictures. When Hope had first moved in, after the Viscount was first committed to debtor's prison, there had still been a butler and a single footman to wait on them while they ate. Now, Ruth and Agnes kept no servants beyond a cook and a single, put-upon maid that lived downstairs. There was a light luncheon of cold meat, bread, and butter spread upon the table.

Agnes was waiting. At the age of seventeen, the poor girl ought to be preparing for her coming-out. She was dark-haired and dark-eyed, and pretty enough to catch a fairly decent man, if she could enter the marriage mart during the Season. Of course, that was unlikely to ever happen. The Viscount was supposed to be financing her first Season. Coming Out was expensive, horribly so, and the simple fact was that Ruth and Agnes could not afford it. Hope had nurtured some fantasies of saving up every penny she earned and somehow having a half-decent stash of savings to put towards Agnes' coming out.

That was a silly dream, she could see that now. Nobody could afford even the cheapest of London Seasons on a governess' wage.

And, of course, there was the small issue of Hope having no employment at all.

Until now.

"I have a position." Hope announced, setting down the paper on the table. "A gentleman has applied to the agency to provide him with a governess and has left it up to their discretion who is chosen. Mr Swill informed me that they're willing to take a chance on me, and my lack of references is unlikely to come up. So, I have a position. I'm to start in four days' time, once the gentleman is informed."

Agnes gave a gasp. "Oh, that's wonderful news, Hope! You've been waiting for so long."

"It's so sudden." Ruth murmured. "Darling, are you sure about taking up this position? If a gentleman applies, that could mean that there's no lady of the house on the scene. That can be a good thing or a bad thing, you know. You can stay with us."

A lump rose to Hope's throat. She knew, and had known since the day she arrived, that her aunt could barely afford to keep her. Without Hope here, they could save up a little money, plus whatever Hope could afford to pay back. They'd never resented her, not even for a moment.

Hope reached across the table to take her aunt's hand, then Agnes'.

"I'm going." She said firmly. "If all goes well, I'll leave this position with a good reference. Then, getting another position will be very easy."

"I suppose so." Ruth said doubtfully.

"Who is the gentleman?" Agnes asked. "Is it anyone we would know?"

"Well, the name is familiar, but I can't think from where. I shall be working for the Duke of Darenwood."

"Goodness." Ruth murmured. "Now there's a name to think on."

Chapter Two

Four Days Later

The dream was more or less the same as it always was. Some people reported being able to control their dreams, and do whatever they pleased in them, but Ewan had never had that skill.

In the dream, he was racing along a corridor. A familiar corridor, a long, thin one that had no windows, and some truly ugly wallpaper that Caroline had always inexplicably liked. He was running as fast as he could, his lungs screaming for air, vision swimming, a painful stitch stabbing at his sides. He wasn't making any forward progress, though. Not a single inch.

He could see Caroline's bedroom ahead, the door closed, and he somehow Ewan knew that if he didn't reach it in time, it would be too late and she would be dead, with Lucas lying beside her, cold as ice.

The corridor seemed to shrink and elongate, the door drawing further and further away, and yet the handle was only inches from his fingertips.

Inches, but it might as well have been miles, as Ewan could not touch it.

Ewan woke with a start, sitting bolt upright. He struggled to catch his breath, squeezing his eyes closed and centering himself. He was in his own room, of course, the bed sheets tangled around him, the air still and cool.

He squinted through the crack in the curtains, estimating that the hour was around half past six in the morning. So, he would usually be getting up in about half an hour, anyway.

No point going back to sleep now.

Ewan flopped back into the pillows, letting his pounding heart calm down. The weather was unseasonably cold for the time of year, yet sweat beaded on his forehead, pooling uncomfortably under his nightshirt.

He hadn't slept well since he lost Caroline. Worries and regrets plagued him nightly – what if he'd called the doctor that first evening, when she first felt unwell? There'd been no reason to suspect that she was suffering from anything more than a little tiredness. They'd taken Lucas on a day trip to the lake, and Caroline was tired when they returned. None of them had even thought twice about it.

Would it have made any difference? Ewan would never know now. The fever had set in by the morning and progressed quickly. Very quickly, and he could console himself with that knowledge. She hadn't suffered.

She'd left her husband and son behind to suffer without her, instead. It was hard not to feel resentful. That was foolish, Ewan knew, but he conversely blamed Caroline for leaving him to bring up Lucas alone, and plough through life without her. Of course it wasn't her fault, but it wasn't as if Ewan was capable of thinking rationally at the moment.

Sometimes he could hardly believe that she'd been gone for two years. Some days it felt as though he'd only just lost her.

The door opened, and Ewan's valet appeared.

"Good morning, your Grace." He said politely, moving directly over to the window to throw open the curtains.

Sixsmith was a short, slim young man with a mane of red hair. Some of his previous employers had insisted that he wear hair-powder to cover the outrageous shade of red, but Ewan thought that was ridiculous. Perhaps his easy-going attitude was why Sixsmith, one of the most valued valets around, had stayed with him for so long.

"Good morning, Sixsmith." Ewan mumbled, squinting against the sharp grey light streaming in through the window. "What time is it, by the way?"

"Quarter to seven, your Grace. I heard movement in your room, so I thought I would slip in a little early."

"That's very convenient, thank you. Is anyone else awake yet?"

"Her Grace, the Dowager Duchess, has come down, and I believe young Master Lucas will be up soon."

"I see. Well, I have work to do on the estate, and only two days to complete it in. I can't say I'm looking forward to returning to London."

Sixsmith made a vague noise of sympathy. "Your Grace, you have received a reply from the employment agency. It arrived this morning."

He handed over a neat white fold of paper, sealed with a somewhat ostentatious blob of red wax. Ewan didn't particularly like the employment agency he'd chosen, but they were highly rated, and known to produce very competent and reliable governesses.

That was what Ewan needed. Efficient, reliable, and calm. Somebody who could manage Lucas and put up with his grandmother's constant interfering. He'd already had to get rid of his last two governesses at her request.

Request was rather a light and inoffensive word. Demand was probably more accurate.

Ewan tore open the letter and read quickly, propped up against the pillows while Sixsmith bustled around the room, getting things ready.

"They haven't said much about her." Ewan commented. "Normally they're waxing poetical about the woman's accomplishments and achievements. Did they send references along with her? They usually do. As if listing all the lords and ladies the poor woman has worked for will make me impressed."

"I daresay that works on many people." Sixsmith said tactfully. "No, your Grace. There were no additional documents."

"Hm. Strange. Still, never mind. The others had a pile of references at least an inch thick, and they all left. She's to meet us in London, it says. I do hope she lasts."

Sixsmith said nothing. Ewan glanced over at his valet, the very picture of discretion and reliability, and suppressed a smile. Sixsmith didn't approve of the constant chopping and changing of governesses, and he also didn't approve of the Dowager's interference. Not that he'd be so bold as to say it, of course.

Ewan didn't blame him. Much as he appreciated his mother's help, he knew that she could be a little... well, a little overbearing. She'd suggested more than once that he dismiss Sixsmith and bring in somebody more 'suitable'. He had no idea what sort of 'suitability' she meant and couldn't imagine anyone better suited to his work than Sixsmith in any case.

No doubt the valet had heard what she said and felt for her accordingly. It didn't bother Ewan too much. While he might listen to his mother's suggestions as to the governesses he hired, he had no intention of losing his valet to her interfering.

He climbed out of bed, tossing the letter aside. It really didn't make much difference to him which governess was sent. They were all more or less the same – clever, patient women, who liked children and were keen to earn a living. He prided himself on offering a less distasteful placement than some other houses – what with their spoilt children and leering fathers and brothers – and hadn't had any real cause to dislike any of the governesses so far.

His mother, of course, had a very different opinion on the situation. Very different.

***

"Good morning, Mother." Ewan said, stepping into the drawing room. "You're up early."

The Dowager Duchess of Darenwood, Lady Margaret Spencer, was sitting in state in her favourite armchair, angled towards the fire. She was strong and healthy despite her age and was one of those rare women who looked very fine in black silks and satin, decorated with pearls and black lace. She'd taken very well to being a widow.

"I thought I would make the most of our time in the country." Margaret said with a sigh. "Before we go back to London and fill our lungs with that awful, thick air. Miasmas are terrible for the health, you know. Can't we stay another few weeks?"

"I'm afraid not, Mother." Ewan bent to kiss Margaret's papery cheek. "I have to get back. Besides, the new governess is meeting us in London. I just received news this morning."

Margaret pressed her lips together. "Please tell me that you haven't got another of those silly girls from the agency."

Ewan winced, settling himself in the opposite armchair. Lucas was curled up on the rug in front of the fire, absorbed in a picture book. He hadn't yet noticed his father's presence, much to Ewan's amusement.

"I have, but I'm sure this one will do quite well."

Margaret made a little moue of displeasure. "Really, Ewan, I wish you wouldn't bother. They never have any substance. Do you know, the last woman you hired had no understanding of Algebra at all? Or trigonometry. How is she meant to properly educate our son if even the simplest forms of Mathematics elude her?"

"I think that calling Algebra and trigonometry the simplest forms of Mathematics are somewhat unfair." Ewan pointed out gently.

"Yes, but we want Lucas to have a proper, well-rounded education, do we not?"

"Of course, but he's only six years old."

They turned to inspect Lucas. He was the very image of his father, with coffee-brown curls and matching chocolate-coloured eyes. He was a sweet little boy, and very good-natured. He got that from his mother, although Ewan sometimes wished that his son looked a little more like Caroline. It would be good to see some traces of her face there.

Lucas turned around, smiling sweetly.

"Good morning, Papa."

"Good morning, Lucas. Did you sleep well?"

Lucas considered this. He was a softly spoken boy, with a tendency to think long and hard before he spoke. Now that was a trait he had learned from Ewan, although he didn't seem to have inherited his father's temper, at least.

"Yes, Papa, I did."

"Excellent. Did you hear what I said to Grandmother just now? You'll be getting a new governess when we return to London."

This news didn't seem to please Lucas very much.

"I liked Miss Mullins."

Margaret snorted. "Miss Mullins was an impertinent chit of a girl. Always talking back, always questioning, always contradicting me. She had the silliest ways of teaching the poor boy. Thank heavens she had the sense to leave when she did. I was starting to believe that you would never have dismissed her."

Ewan carefully said nothing. The subject of Miss Mullins, the latest in a long line of governesses, was a sore one. Miss Mullins had been a cheerful, round-faced woman of about thirty, with a decided knack for children. Lucas had taken to her immediately and seemed to thrive on her unusual and unique teaching style.

Ewan personally did not mind what style of teaching the governesses used, so long as it worked with Lucas. His mother took an immediate dislike to the woman and set about making her life a misery. It wasn't a surprise when Miss Mullins handed in her notice only three months later.

Frankly, Ewan was surprised that she'd lasted that long. He'd written her a glowing reference, much to Margaret's annoyance. He did his best to stop his mother putting such pressure on the governesses, but really, he couldn't be in two places at once. If he could just find a governess that his mother liked too, everything would be fine.

After all, she had Lucas' best interests at heart.

"I hope you'll be a little nicer to this next governess, Mother." He said firmly. "No interfering, no making her feel uncomfortable."

"I won't hold back if I find her lacking in any way. You know me, Ewan. I speak as I find, and I despise dishonesty. So, who has this governess worked for before? Anyone we know?"

"I don't know." Ewan replied, leaning forward to ruffle Lucas' hair. The little boy had gone back to reading his book and seemed entirely content. "The agency didn't say."

There was a tense silence.

"They didn't say? Well, that's unusual." Margaret commented, her voice tight. "What about her references?"

"They didn't send any."

Margaret straightened up a little more, obviously outraged. "Well, that's disgraceful, Ewan. Did you write back to them immediately, and request that the references be forwarded to you?"

"No, Mother, I didn't."

"Well, you ought to hurry, otherwise they'll say that it's too late and she's already on her way. Really, Ewan, must I do everything for you?"

Ewan felt a stab of irritation. He drew in a few deep breaths and reminded himself to be calm and patient with his mother. After all, she'd been there when he lost Caroline. She'd supported him when he was left with a three-year-old child and a sense of being unmoored in rough seas. Perhaps Margaret was a little too involved in his household dealings, but she could be forgiven that, couldn't she?

"I asked the agency to pick out someone suitable." Ewan

said, once his temper had quelled. "They know my situation, and they recommended this particular woman very highly."

Margaret made a brief, dismissive gesture, waving away all of the agency's experience and expertise with a flick of her wrist.

"That doesn't matter. What if... what if this woman doesn't have any references?"

Ewan cleared his throat. "Lucas, is Emily in the nursery?"

Lucas glanced over his shoulder. "Yes, Papa."

"Well, why don't you go up and see her for a moment? Your grandmother and I want to talk about something."

Lucas nodded, marking his place in his book and tucking it under his arm. He scrambled to his feet, pausing to kiss Margaret and then Ewan on the cheek, and slipped out into the hallway.

"That's another thing." Margaret said, once the door had closed behind him. "Lucas has Emily. If he already has a nursemaid, why does he need a governess?"

"Emily is a nursemaid. That means that it's her responsibility to feed him, dress him, and so on. She's like a valet for children. A governess will teach him and help him learn the difference between right and wrong, and so forth. It's not fair to expect Emily to do both."

Margaret tutted. "Well, how about this. We'll find a suitable governess – I shall pick out someone – and dismiss Emily. That way, the governess can do all of those things at once. We'll save money."

Another flare of irritation rushed through Ewan. He distracted himself by picking at his cuffs, turning his cufflinks round and round. They were a present from Caroline years ago, if he remembered correctly.

"I'm not dismissing Emily. That isn't fair."

"You are too sentimental, Ewan."

"Lucas would be upset. She's been with us since he was a baby."

"He'll recover."

Ewan pressed his lips together and glanced away. He was aware of his mother's eyes on him, watching and waiting for him to give in. He usually did give in, just to stop Margaret talking and talking and talking about the subject. She knew just how to wear a person down. Caroline had a similar skill. Perhaps that was why she and Margaret had gotten on so well. Ewan studiously avoided her gaze.

Finally, when it was clear that Ewan was not going to reply, Margaret sighed, shaking her head.

"You've made up your mind. I see. Well, I shan't push my advice onto you, Ewan. I just hope that we don't live to regret it. It sounds to me like this young woman has no references, in which case she'll no doubt be a disaster."

"Perhaps it's her first position."

"Oh, goodness, don't say such things!" Margaret drew her shawl tighter around herself and shuddered. "Her first position. We certainly don't want the scrapings from the top of the stew, do we?"

Ewan wasn't entirely sure what that meant and didn't care to ask.

"Well, how else is she meant to collect references?"

Margaret gave a small, vague shrug, indicating that she did not know, and furthermore, she did not care.

"I really shouldn't know, dearest. With other families, I suppose. Less noble families, who don't much care about hiring proper governesses. It's clear that your mind is made up, and the girl is coming."

"I'm afraid that my mind is made up, Mother. You shouldn't have to worry about this sort of thing. Just concentrate on being Lucas' grandmother, rather than being his nursemaid, governess, and mother all rolled into one. You do enough for us. I wish you wouldn't worry so much about us all."

Margaret was quiet for a long moment.

"I like to think that Caroline would be pleased to know that I'm here, taking charge of things." She said carefully, twisting the hem of her shawl into tight little rolls. "When it comes to household problems – governesses, for one thing – gentlemen like yourself really can't know how to go about it. It isn't your fault, dearest." She reached over, patting Ewan's knee. "But fear not. I shall be here, and I shall watch this new governess with the eyes of a hawk. Nothing she does will slip past me, I can assure you. And she'll find me very unforgiving."

"Of course, Mother." Ewan said, because it seemed like the quickest way to end the conversation.

Chapter Three

"Are we there yet, Papa?" Lucas asked, yawning and stretching.

Ewan smiled fondly at his son. "I'm afraid not, Lucas. You've been exceptionally well-behaved, though. Not many young boys would be so still and patient, cooped up in a carriage like you have been."

Lucas beamed back at his father, pride shining out of his young face.

Ewan was not exaggerating. They had been on the road for close to three days now. He could have travelled faster by himself, of course, but with the slow pace they had to take for Margaret's comfort and the regular stops at inns, their journey had stretched out interminably.

Margaret had been uncharacteristically quiet. Ewan had been braced for a barrage of complaints, a fresh wave coming every time they set off from another inn. Margaret was never happy with the places they stayed.

But there had been hardly any complaints at all. For the most part, Margaret had sat quietly in her seat opposite, looking out of the window, and occasionally playing card games with her son and grandson.

"I know you aren't looking forward to London, Mother, but it's a convenient place." Ewan said, when the silence stretched out a little too long. "The move and the travel are a nuisance, of course, but once we're there and settled, you will feel much better."

Margaret flashed a tight smile. "I'm sure. And when are we meeting the latest disaster of a governess?"

"Oh, Mother. Please don't be like that. I want her to feel welcome."

"Will I like my new governess as much as I liked Miss Mullins?" Lucas asked dubiously. "Miss Mullins was very nice."

"Yes, I remember, Lucas."

"Why did she leave, Papa? She would never tell me. I cried and cried when she said that she was leaving."

Ewan glanced reproachfully over Lucas' head at his mother.

He wasn't sure what he was expecting to find. A flash of guilt, perhaps? A sense of understanding over what she'd done?

There was nothing like that, of course.

"The woman was entirely unsuitable." Margaret said blandly, patting the top of Lucas' head. "You don't understand now, dearest, because you are too small. One day, however, you'll understand. You'll realize that Miss Mullins was not a suitable person for you to spend time with, and that's that."

"Why wasn't she suitable?" Lucas asked at once.

Margaret hesitated, missing a beat. "Well, she didn't do things properly. She didn't stick to your schoolbooks the way she should and had very strange ideas about things. I remember overhearing her once say that women ought to be able to vote, just like men. Can you imagine, Ewan?"

Lucas frowned harder. "Why can't ladies vote?"

Margaret gave a little huff of laughter. "Do you see, Ewan? Do you see how that woman has influenced her? I wanted her dismissed the day I overheard that nonsense. Reason with your son, please."

Ewan glanced down at his son, who was looking up at him with a mixture of curiosity and outrage. Lucas had reached that age when he was starting to realize that all was not fair with the world, and he was keen to remedy that.

"There are some men in the world who don't believe that women are proper people. They think that they are not as good as men." Ewan said simply. "Those people do not want women to hold power, and being able to vote is a kind of power."

Lucas digested this. "Are women proper people?"

"Well, what do you think?"

"I think so. Miss Mullins and Emily are proper people, and so is Grandmother."

"Well reasoned. Do you believe your Grandmother is somehow less intelligent than, say, me?"

Lucas shook his head vigorously. "Not at all."

"Indeed. People are people, regardless of what they look like, or where they were born, or indeed who they were born as. We are all made equal, and we ought to be treated the same. What do you think of that?"

"I think that it is fair."

"I concur."

Margaret, who had pressed a handkerchief over her mouth in horror for most of this speech, shook her head.

"This is not funny, Ewan." She snapped.

"I am not joking. Do you want your grandson to grow up believing that you are less of a person? Or that his wife is somehow inferior to him, or his daughters?"

"That is not at all the same thing."

Ewan only smiled, not keen to keep up the argument. "I think you'll find it is, Mother. But no matter. We'll soon be in London, then we can all get out of this tiresome carriage and rest. Won't that be nice, Lucas."

Lucas nodded, smiling. "Can we visit the Royal Menagerie when we're there? And the Tower of London?"

"Of course we can. Mother, would you like to come with us when we visit?"

Margaret sighed. "Perhaps. Good Lord, I'm tired of travelling. I do wish we could have just stayed in the country."

Perhaps it was Ewan's frazzled nerves that made him snap more than was proper.

"Well, Mother, you are well within your rights to commandeer a carriage and take yourself back there, if you like."

Margaret blinked, pressing her lips together. "Goodness. I daresay you'll soon have no need for me at all, if you haven't decided so already."

Ewan sucked in a breath. "That's not what I mean, Mother. Not at all."

She said nothing, glancing out of the window, and an uncomfortable silence sprung up between them.

Ewan felt guilty. He shouldn't have spoken to his mother like that. The carriage journey was fraying his nerves too. There was nothing to be done but to sit and think. He'd finished the book he brought during the first day of their trip, and since then there'd been nothing to do but chat languidly and think about all the tasks that awaited him at home. They had a pack of cards, of course, but there were really only so many games of cards a person could play. Besides, they were limited to three players at most, and Lucas only had the patience for simple card games.

Once again, Ewan's mind slipped back to the governess. He

had liked Miss Mullins, but what if they hired somebody who did hold objectionable beliefs? What if she was a poor governess? What then?

Oh, Caroline, Ewan thought miserably. Am I doing the right thing? If you were here, you would have picked out the governess yourself. It would have been as easy to you as breathing. You would have interviewed her and gotten her measure right away, and that would be that. Mother wouldn't have been able to browbeat you.

He leaned back in his seat and closed his eyes, praying that they'd reach home soon.

***

Hope surveyed her paltry wardrobe with a frown.

Over the years, her clothes had become irreplaceable. Not in terms of sentimentality or expense, but in sheer practicality. New dresses were expensive, and the newer fashions required yards and yards of extra fabric, which she simply could not afford. The clothes remaining were well cared for, washed gently, and darned in multiple places.

While she had packed the essentials – underclothes, night things, stockings, petticoats, and so on – Hope had not yet packed any of her dresses. She'd laid them all out on her bed, and was currently staring at her selection, waiting for something to happen.

Two dresses were fine ballgowns, remnants of an easier, more pleasant time of life. There'd be no need for those where she was going, so Hope had set them aside.

But what about her everyday clothes? There was, of course, no question of buying new dresses, and she could not possibly bring them all. Once she was established in her new position and saving up her earnings, Hope might be able to buy some new fabric, but when would she have time to make herself a new dress? Besides, what would the family think of her if she did?

Try and she might, Hope couldn't recollect any of her friends' governesses. It was years ago, of course. Some ladies were sent to finishing schools at sixteen, and so a governess would no longer be needed. Some families preferred deportment teachers, dancing masters, singing masters, and so on, rather than one put-upon governess who might come to have too much influence over their precious child.

This did not help.

Hope sighed, raking a hand through her hair. A gentle knock on the door made her jump.

"It's me." Ruth poked her head around the door. "How is the packing going? Ah." She added, taking in the chaos, piles of clothes everywhere. "Not well, I see."

"I truly don't know what to take. Aunt Ruth. I daresay I'm just fussing over nothing."

"I don't think so." Ruth said, pushing open the door and stepping inside. "First impressions are very important, and this family will be watching you closely."

A frisson of fear rolled down Hope's spine. She had considered this, of course. She was going to teach the only son of a duke, a child who would be incredibly precious to his family. Of course all eyes would be on her, and they would likely not be kind ones.

"I don't think I can do this." Hope mumbled.

Ruth did not flinch. "Of course you can, my dear. Now, let me see. You don't want to bring anything fancy. No point in ballgowns for a governess, I'm afraid. I see you've set those aside. Now, your employers will likely expect you to dress sedately and plainly. A good governess is meant to blend in with the furniture, I'm afraid. That means you should select plain, staid dresses."

Ruth leaned over the bed, picking up a dull brown dress with a plain lace collar, and a dove-grey one. After a moment's hesitation, she selected a third dress, a darker grey than the second. Hope didn't even remember when she'd bought those dresses – during better times, perhaps – and they were generally thought to be too plain and ugly to wear in Society. She would never wear them to a party, to be sure.

"I suppose you're right, Aunt." Hope conceded. "But what if there's some sort of occasion? A dinner party, perhaps, or an outing of some kind, and I am expected to go? I suppose that if the little boy is going, I will have to go."

"That is an excellent point. I suggest that you bring one extra dress, one for best. How about this lavender gown? It's plain and sensible, but such a pretty colour."

Hope nodded. "Yes, that would do. Thank you, Aunt."

"Not at all, my dear." Ruth said, carefully sweeping away the rest of the dresses. "The rest of your clothes will stay here, so you can come back and get them whenever you please, don't fret. Four dresses is a good number to be getting on with. Now, some advice. When you get to where you are going, try and find out what your position will be."

"My position?"

"Yes, my dear. A governess is placed awkwardly in the household – not at the level of the family, of course, but certainly above the average servant. You may be expected to eat in the kitchen, or in your rooms, or even with the family. The servants might be tasked with doing your laundry, or you may be expected to do your own. Do you see what I mean? Position is important."

Hope swallowed hard, nodding. She'd understood, of course, that she would be in a precarious position in her new home – but just how precarious remained to be seen.

"I understand, Aunt."

Ruth eyed her for a long moment. "I hope that you do, my darling girl. Remember that your place relies on the goodwill of the family, but don't be so foolish as to lord it over the other servants. Not that you would, of course. Make friends, Hope. Make friends quickly. Keep your counsel, keep your temper in check, and for heaven's sake, make sure the little boy likes you."

Hope sat down heavily on the edge of the bed. Her heart was pounding, and she felt sick and dizzy. It was all real. It was really happening. She was going to strike out on her own, and who only knew what would come of it?

"I'm afraid, Aunt Ruth." She said quietly. "There must have been plenty of other ladies suitable for this position. What if I am a terrible disappointment? I could make a mistake and not realize, and then…"

"Calm down, my dear girl." Ruth soothed, sitting beside her. "You worry entirely too much. I'm sure you will do perfectly well, but even if you don't, you can always come back here, can't you? This is your home. We'll keep your room for you and keep your clothes here. Everything will be fine."

Hope forced a smile. Her aunt was kind, so kind, but Hope knew, deep down, that there would be no coming back. She'd already drained enough of her aunt and cousin's money and future. Now, Hope needed to strike out on her own and pay back some of what she owed.

The relief was still there, simmering underneath the fear. Relief that she had finally secured a position, a real opportunity to earn money and pay her own way in the world.

Not, of course, that Hope could say any of this to her aunt. She glanced up, meeting her aunt's eye, and forced a smile.

"Of course, Aunt Ruth. Of course. You're very kind, both of you. Now, I daresay I should finish packing before we get started on supper, what do you think?"

Chapter Four

"Home sweet home." Ewan remarked, as the eaves of their townhouse popped into view.

He wished he hadn't said that. It sounded hollow. It was the sort of thing Caroline might have said as they arrived home, her voice soft and playful, and he would have laughed and agreed with her. Now, though, the words sounded like a badly phrased joke.

Margaret was still not speaking to him. Lucas, always alert to changes around him, was glancing warily from one to another. He clearly did not understand what was going on but knew that there was a frosty atmosphere between his father and grandmother.

The carriage lurched to a halt, and Ewan clambered out with relief, subtly stretching out his cramped limbs. It had been rather too cold to open the window, and anyway Margaret would have complained about a draft. He drew in deep lungfuls of fresh, clean air, reveling in it. This was London, of course, so the air was not as clean and pleasant as the countryside, but it was markedly better than the stale, warm air inside the carriage.

Sixsmith leapt nimbly from where he and Emily had been sitting beside the coachman. He held up his arms to help her down, and she beamed at him. Ewan suppressed a smile. He'd long since thought that Emily and Sixsmith were extremely friendly with each other but was careful not to mention his suspicions. Margaret was very keen on the servants not having followers and might try and dismiss one or both of them.

It was late in the day, and the sun was already below the horizon. The house was lit up in preparation for their return, warm and inviting. Margaret clambered out of the carriage behind him, and Lucas bounced down, slipping his small hand into his father's.

The servants were lined up on the front steps to meet them, the butler and housekeeper at the very end. They were a married couple, Mr and Mrs Golightly.

"Goodness, Golightly, Mrs Golightly, what are you thinking, dragging the servants out in this chill night air to greet us?" Ewan said, laughing. "The poor things! Get yourselves into the warm at once, and that is an order."

The servants bobbed curtseys and flashed smiles, relieved to get out of the cold. The butler and housekeeper stepped forward to greet Ewan, both smiling. As some middle-aged couples tended to do, they now looked rather similar. They had the same silvery-black hair, cheerful round faces, and pudgy, stocky bodies. They had worked for Ewan's grandfather and grandmother before him, and even Margaret respected them enough not to poke holes in their work.

"Welcome home, your Graces, and young Master Lucas." Golightly said, bowing. "A light supper has been prepared."

"Ah, perfect, thank you. I think Master Lucas will be retiring to bed. Could you take him up, Emily? I shall come up to say goodnight before he goes to sleep."

"Certainly, your Grace." Emily said, coming forward and extending her hand to Lucas. He took it with a smile, and the two skipped off into the depths of the house. Sixsmith had already melted away, no doubt hurrying off to Ewan's room to unpack everything and set everything straight.

"Mother, could I have a word with you, please?" Ewan said, as Margaret slipped past him into the hall. "It's important. Mrs Golightly, could we eat our supper in my study? Assuming the room is ready, of course."

"The room is indeed ready, your Grace." Mrs Golightly said, faintly offended that a room would not be ready for us under her leadership. "Supper will be served in fifteen minutes."

"Perfect. Thank you, all of you."

The last of the servants melted away, leaving Ewan and Margaret alone in the hallway. Ewan suddenly realized how badly he wanted to change and enjoy a long, hot soak in a bathtub. The inns were never clean enough, and he felt grimy and itchy, his clothes stiff and travel soiled.

But this business with Margaret had to be dealt with, as soon as possible.

She raised an eyebrow. "Do I have a choice, or am I being summoned?"

Ewan rolled his eyes. "You are my mother. I can't summon you anywhere. But I would like to talk to you. Please."

Margaret sighed. "Very well. I can spare a few minutes. I don't want supper, all that travelling has taken my appetite."

The study was freshly cleaned, smelling of polish and books. The floor was scrubbed to a high shine, and there was scarcely a mote of dust in the air. In anticipation of their arrival, a roaring fire had been built up in the grate. Ewan indicated the two armchairs set before the fireplace, and Margaret sat down with a happy sigh, warming her hands.

"I don't particularly like London, but I'm glad that we're here at last." She conceded. "Now. What was it you wanted?"

Ewan drew in a deep breath. "I'm sorry, Mother. I spoke sharply to you in the carriage today, and I am sorry for that. It's not an excuse, but I was tired and aching and sick of travelling. We all were, I know. I didn't mean to suggest that you should go back to the country. As to my having no use for you – well, you're my mother and Lucas' grandmother, not a servant, so you don't need to be useful at all, but that's not the point. My point is that I don't know what we would have done without you. Even now, I rely on you so heavily at times it scares me."

Margaret visibly softened. "Oh, Ewan, you sweet boy. You needn't apologize. We were all in a bad temper, I think."

"This business with the governess – all of the governesses, actually – is clearly something that's getting between us, and I'm sorry for it."

"I know that the boy needs a governess, but I want him to have someone we can rely on." Margaret said firmly. "I won't apologize for that, but perhaps... well, maybe I have been a little overzealous at times."

Ewan had to smile. "Perhaps. Either way, I wanted to let you know how deeply I appreciate you and what you have done. I shouldn't turn my back on your advice so quickly. As a way of making it up to you, I'd like you to be with us tomorrow, when we meet the governess for the first time."

Margaret chewed her lip. "And am I to keep my opinions to myself?"

"No. In fact..." Ewan paused, taking a breath. Perhaps he was making a mistake, but he'd seen the hurt flash across his mother's face in the carriage. He needed to make amends. "In fact, I have decided that when the governess begins her work, she will report directly to you."

Margaret's face lit up. "Really? That's quite something,

coming from you, Ewan. Are you sure you won't be hanging over my shoulder, watching every decision I make?"

Ewan was not sure at all. "Of course." He said firmly. "I trust you, Mother. I'm going to show you that, once and for all."

Margaret reached out, taking her son's hand.

"I'm glad you talked to me." She said softly. "In the carriage, I did rather feel... well, that I'd outlived my usefulness. Bright young governesses can easily get between an old woman and her beloved grandchild, and it's remarkably easy to feel that control has been neatly wrenched from your hands. Not a pleasant thing for a lady of my age."

"Nonsense. I adore you, Mother, and Lucas certainly does. Governess or not, you will always be Lucas' grandmother, and my own mother. Always. Remember that."

"Either way, I'm glad we talked about this. I shall take this business with the governess seriously, I promise you. I do understand that this constant switching of governesses cannot be good for Lucas, and after all, we should only be thinking about his wellbeing."

"I couldn't agree more." Ewan said, relieved. "So, you aren't going to dismiss the poor governess on a pretext?"

"No, I shan't. Now, I won't hold back if she is somehow lacking, but I promise you that I shall give her a fair chance, at least."

She smiled at him, and Ewan smiled back. A feeling of relief was creeping through his chest. It did feel good to unload his worry about the governess onto his mother's shoulders, after all.

***

"Is he asleep?" Ewan asked softly, hovering outside Lucas' room.

Emily, who was in the process of sneaking out of the door, shook her head.

"Not yet, your Grace. Almost, though. I just finished reading him his bedtime story, but he is waiting for you to go in and say goodnight."

That made Ewan's heart ache. He'd spent longer talking to Margaret than he'd planned, and then there was supper. It was easy to forget the small promises you made to a child, but the children didn't forget.

Still, he was here now.

Ewan slipped into the dark nursery, lit up by a single candle set on the nightstand beside Lucas' bed.

"Your Grace?" Emily whispered, peering through the crack of the door. "Will you blow out the candle once you are finished?"

"Of course."

She nodded, closing the door softly after him.

Lucas was huddled in his bed, pushed into a corner of the nursery. The candle flickered and guttered, burned down to a stub. The rest of the room was thrown into deep shadow, abandoned toys and playthings throwing unusual dark shapes across the floor and against the wall. A bookcase was reduced to a smear of darkness in the corner.

"Papa?" Lucas asked sleepily, a tiny lump under the swathe of blankets and pillows. "Emily read me my bedtime story."

"Yes, darling, I'm sorry. I was talking to your Grandmama."

Lucas blinked, shifting in bed. "Is she still cross?"

"Not anymore, no."

Ewan perched on the side of the bed, leaning forward. Lucas' face was slack with sleep, his eyes struggling to stay open. In this light, he looked even younger. Not for the first time, Ewan felt a pang of misery that Caroline was not here to se him.

"I'm glad." Lucas yawned.

"So am I. Now, listen to me, Lucas. I'm sure you know that your new governess is arriving tomorrow. Are you excited?"

Lucas considered. "I don't think that I am excited. I'm interested in meeting her, though. Will she want to teach me Algebra? Grandmama said that all my governesses should be teaching me Algebra."

"I don't think she will, no. Of course, if you feel like you want to learn Algebra..."

"I don't." Lucas said, with feeling.

Ewan chuckled, reaching out to ruffle his hair.

"Very well, then. You need to be honest with me about how well you like this governess. Your Grandmama will be watching her, and we'll all wait and see how well you get along. How does that sound?"

Lucas nodded obediently. "Grandmama doesn't like any of my governesses, though."

"Well, she has promised to give this one a fair shot. There is another thing, too. I want you, Lucas, to be on your very best behaviour when we meet this lady. We don't want her thinking that you're a little hooligan, do we?"

Lucas looked horrified, as if hooliganism was simply the worst thing a person could ever be. No doubt in his six-year-old mind, it was.

"Why would she think I was a hooligan, Papa?"

"Well, if you don't eat your dinner properly, or if you don't mind your lessons. That's the sort of thing hooligans do."

Lucas nodded obediently. "I shall be on my very, very best behaviour, Papa. My nicest, shiniest behaviour."

Ewan smiled. "That's exactly what I want to hear."

He paused, looking down at his son. It was obvious that Lucas was entirely exhausted. If the long trip had left Ewan and Margaret so tired, goodness only knew what it would have done to the little boy. His eyes were rolling, he was so tired, and he seemed to sink further into the mattress and pillows with every breath.

And yet Ewan wanted to stay there forever. He wanted to sweep Lucas into his arms and hold him close. They could go to sleep like that, just like they had when Lucas was smaller and after Caroline had just died, and the only comfort Ewan could find was from holding his beloved son.

Then Lucas gave an almighty yawn, stretching his arms above his head.

"Can you blow out the candle, Papa?" he asked sleepily. "I don't like the shadows."

Ewan smiled sadly down at him. "Of course, sweetheart."

He bent down to press a kiss to Lucas' forehead, then blew out the candle in one swift movement.

The nursery was enveloped in darkness, leaving Ewan to pick his way to the door blind.

Lucas was growing up, he supposed. Soon he wouldn't want goodnight kisses and bedtime stories from his papa. Soon he wouldn't need a nursemaid and governess at all. Try and he might, Ewan could not remember much about his own nursemaid, except that she was a jolly woman with strong arms.

When did time begin to race? And how on earth could Ewan start to claw it back?

He couldn't, of course, but it was nice to pretend.

Ewan reached the door without tripping over on discarded toys and slipped open the door. A beam of light from the hall outside trickled into the room, and he glanced back at Lucas.

The little boy was already fast asleep.

Chapter Five

The Following Day

It was raining hard outside, and that seemed to be appropriate.

"Do you have everything?" Ruth said, her voice artificially bright. "It doesn't matter if you forget a thing or two, we can always send it on to you."

Hope smiled weakly. "Yes, of course. Thank you, Aunt Ruth."

Agnes was leaning against the hallway wall, arms wrapped around herself, eyeing Hope's bags and boxes with a doleful expression.

"I can't believe that you're really going." She murmured. "I suppose I thought… oh, I don't know what I thought. That some magical solution would present itself, I suppose."

"Agnes, really." Ruth tutted. "None of us want Hope to leave, but the sad fact is that sometimes people have to go out into the world and earn a living. She has an excellent position in a very fine house, and we ought to be grateful for that. She will earn a decent wage…"

"I'll send money home." Hope blurted. "No, Aunt Ruth, please, you must let me send some of my wages home. I'll be very careful and diligently save up the rest, but I would feel much better if I knew that you and Agnes are living a little more comfortably. You've done so much for me over the years. It's the very least I can do."

Ruth opened her mouth then closed it again, her eyes filling with tears.

"You are a sweet, kind girl, Hope. Of course we'll accept whatever money you can afford to send back. I won't lie, it will come in tremendously handy."

She took out a handkerchief, delicately dabbing her eyes. Agnes was sniffling miserably, and Hope was fighting not to cry. If she cried, her face would go red and blotchy and her eyes would swell, and she wanted to look her best for the first meeting with her employers.

"I had better go, then." Hope said, her voice quavering. "I

don't want to be late on my first day."

"No, of course not, my darling girl. Agnes, will you go and start putting Hope's bags into the hack? I just want to have a quick word with her."

Agnes sniffled again, pocketed her handkerchief, and picked up a bag in each hand. She waddled towards the hired hack waiting outside, with a bored driver picking his nails on the driving seat.

"Listen to me, Hope." Ruth said, quietly and urgently. "You do indeed have a good position, and I have no doubt at all that you can conduct yourself very well. But you must take care of your safety and your reputation. Now you're going out into the world as a working woman, and this can be dangerous. I hear that the Duke of Darenwood is a young man, and a widower. Try and keep your distance from him, if you can. I'm sure he's an entirely honorable gentleman, but the fact is that some noblemen are not honorable. Most gentlemen would not dare trifle with a lady of the ton, for fear of reprisals and scandal. However, you are no longer a lady of the ton. You are a governess. A servant, almost, and men will see you differently. Do you understand what I am saying?"

Hope did, unfortunately. A shiver rolled down her spine.

"I've packed plain and unobtrusive dresses, the ones you recommended. I don't even have any rosewater for perfume, or any jewels."

Ruth shook her head. "This isn't a Society ball, my dear. None of that matters. You're a beautiful young woman, and that is not a helpful thing in your position. Beauty makes people look twice. Now, I'm sure that your position will be entirely secure and the Duke a fine, upstanding gentleman. However, be careful. You will be careful, won't you, darling?"

"I will, Aunt Ruth."

"And beware of gentlemen who seem to profess real affection for you. You are used to being a lady, and so you expect that gentlemen will keep their word. Well, they won't. They may lead you to believe that they love you, that they wish to marry you, but they do not. Never trust anyone, do you hear me?"

Hope felt mildly sick. She hadn't eaten much at breakfast due to her roiling nerves, and now she was glad. She might well have thrown it up.

"I hear you, Aunt Ruth."

"Good. Now, come here and give me a hug. I'm sorry to have shocked you with all of this."

Hope embraced her aunt, pressing her nose into her shoulder.

"Not at all, Aunt. I know you only have my best interests at heart, and I'm glad I have someone to give me advice. I'll miss you both so much."

"And we'll miss you, darling. Now, you really must go. These hired hacks aren't known for getting to their destinations speedily."

Reluctantly, Hope disentangled herself from her aunt. She stepped towards the hack, feeling as though she were moving through a sea of treacle.

Agnes had just finished putting the last bag inside the hack and burst into tears when she found Hope preparing to leave.

There were many goodbyes, tight hugs and kisses, last-minute words of advice and promises to write every week, every day, twice a day.

"Now, now, Agnes, Hope will be very busy." Ruth rebuked gently. "She won't have time to write reams of letters."

"Well, I shall write whenever I can. I promise." Hope vowed solemnly.

Then there was nothing for it but for her to climb into the hack and close the door behind her. The coach smelled stale, the seats hard and uncomfortable, and there was something sticky on the floor. Hope tried not to place the soles of her shoes on it, in case she inadvertently tracked something awful into the Duke of Darenwood's house.

Wouldn't that be mortifying.

With a graceless lurch, the hack shot forward, and Hope was on her way. She twisted to look out of the window at Ruth and Agnes, standing together at the end of the path, looking after her and waving.

Hope waved back, keeping a cheery, reassuring smile on her face. Once her aunt and cousin were out of sight, she sat back against her uncomfortable seat and burst into tears.

***

"We're here, miss." The driver announced bluntly, rapping the head of his cane against the window. Hope flinched, swallowing down the rush of nerves. The hack was an awkward shape, the narrow windows allowing very little view of the surrounding landscape. She hadn't even realized they'd turned into the drive of her destination.

Fiddling with the catch of the door, Hope stumbled gracelessly out into the bright light. It was still raining, fat droplets landing on her bare head. She glanced around, squinting, and saw that the hack had stopped in front of the largest house she'd ever seen. This close up, it was hard to get a real measure of the place beyond a myriad of windows and seemingly endless stone walls sloping up towards the sky. There was a vast garden, muted and veiled by the rain, and a well-raked gravel drive twisting down to the main road. She could see two parallel ruts in the gravel where the hack's wheels had run.

A set of wide stone stairs led up to the main door, which was open. As she watched, two footmen and a portly, middle-aged man came hurrying down, the latter brandishing an umbrella.

"Good day, madam." The man said breezily, opening the umbrella and holding it over her head. "You are the new governess, I assume?"

"I am, yes. Forgive me, I think I am late. We ran into a little traffic in Trafalgar."

The man frowned, glancing at the hack driver. "Trafalgar? Why in the world did you need to go through there?"

The driver shrugged carelessly, offering no explanation. "That'll be two and six, miss."

It was apparent, then, that he'd taken her longer way here, in order to charge for a more expensive trip. If only Hope knew London a little better, she might have said something to him about it.

And then what? She thought. Complain, and end up left on the side of the road with all my bags, in the middle of London?

Blushing, Hope rifled in her reticule for the money, but the man extended one white-gloved hand.

"The bill will be handled madam, don't worry. In the meantime, you can make yourself useful and start taking the luggage out of the hack." He turned to address the hack driver for this last sentence, his voice noticeably colder.

The hack driver scowled. "I don't do that. Passengers handle their own luggage."

"If you wish to be paid, my good sir, you well."

"Now, you look here..."

"No, you look here. You are not bullying a kind-hearted young woman. I am Mr. Golightly, butler to the Duke of Darenwood, and this is his estate. I suggest you fulfil your obligations as soon as possible."

The man blanched. He spun on his heel and began dragging the bags out of the carriage, being sure to bang them around as much as possible.

"Have a care, please!" Mr Golightly snapped. He turned, indicating that Hope should follow him up the stairs. "Now. I apologize for all that unpleasantness. Let's get you inside, where it's warm. The footmen will bring your things to your room. His Grace wished to meet you before anything, however, so follow me."

Hope did so, glad to step into the dry hallway. It was a vast place, large enough to fit Ruth's entire house with ease. She fought to keep herself from gawping up at the painted ceilings and facias. Another footman, wearing glossy emerald-and-gold coloured livery, took her shawl and whisked it away.

"This is a very fine house." Hope said, feeling that she ought to say something. Or perhaps that would mark her out as a silly girl, easily impressed by some nice decoration?

Apparently not. Mr Golightly beamed.

"It is indeed a beautiful building, madam. The housekeeper – my dear wife, Mrs Golightly – will undertake to give you a tour, I'm sure of it. Now, I understand that you are Miss Hope Barlow, is that correct?"

"It is correct. I'm here as a governess for his Grace's son, Master Lucas Darnell?"

"Exactly now. If I may be so bold, the young master is a very sweet boy, and a great favourite with everyone below stairs."

Well, that was a good sign. If all of the household and servants liked the little boy, he probably wasn't a spoilt brat with a raging temper. Hope glanced at her reflection in a gilt mirror, tweaking a few damp strands of hair into place and shaking out her skirts.

Mr Golightly waited tactfully. When she turned back to him, he smiled.

"Shall we go? His Grace is eager to meet you."

"And I am eager to meet him." Hope lied. "Please, lead the way."

Mr Golightly strode along the vast hall ahead of her. His shoes might as well have been shod with velvet – his footsteps made almost no sound at all. Hope's footsteps, on the other hand, rang out and echoed, until she wanted to take them off and just walk in her stockinged feet.

He stopped abruptly before a large, polished mahogany door, and tapped neatly, waiting.

"Come in." came the reply. It was a deep, male voice, one that seemed familiar, although that was probably Hope's panicked brain.

Mr Golightly stepped inside, gesturing for Hope to step in after him.

"The governess has arrived, your Grace. May I introduce Miss Barlow."

The study was dark in comparison to bright, airy hall, and it took Hope a few minutes to adjust. It was a largeish room, obviously designed for comfort and practicality rather than for show. It was an elegant room, but in a thoughtless, effortless sort of way.

There was one other occupant. A man, tall, straight-backed, and broad-shouldered, stood at the window, back turned to her, looking out at the rain.

That, of course, could be none other than the Duke himself.

"Thank you, Golightly." The man said, his voice deep and level. "Please go and inform her Grace the Dowager Duchess that the governess is here."

Mr Golightly bowed, flashed Hope a reassuring smile, and slipped out of the room.

That left them alone. Hope folded her hands in front of her and waited patiently for the man to turn and face her.

He sighed and turned back from the window.

He stopped dead at the sight of her, a frown appearing

between his brows. Recognition jumped across his face at the same moment Hope connected the dots in her mind.

The Duke of Darenwood, a familiar name but nobody she knew. Lucas Darnell.

The face before her had aged, of course. It was a man's face, strong and handsome, rather than a boy's face. The features were so familiar – chocolate brown hands, dark curls, the set of the jaw, the set of the eyebrows.

Hope opened her mouth, the air seeming to have been sucked unceremoniously out of the room.

"Ewan?" she gasped, vaguely aware that addressing a duke by his first name was not a proper form of address.

The Duke of Darenwood – Ewan Darnell – swallowed thickly.

"Hope?" he asked, tentative and shocked. "Is it really you?"

Chapter Six

The memories came flooding back, making Ewan feel almost dizzy. Hope – he ought to call her Miss Barlow now, shouldn't he? – was staring back at him with the same expression of shock and delight that was no doubt on his own face. She was smiling.

How could I ever have forgotten her? Ewan thought wildly. He thought back to the recommendation letter sent by the agency. They'd mentioned Miss Barlow, but it wasn't an uncommon name. Perhaps if they'd said Miss Hope Barlow, that would have triggered his memories.

And then what? Asked a small voice in the back of Ewan's head. Written to them and turned her down? She obviously had no idea it was I that had hired her.

"Ewan?" Hope said, tentatively. "I can't believe it's you. After all these years!"

Ewan swallowed hard, stepping forward. He wanted to pick her up in his arms and swing her around, like they'd done when they were children and Hope was suddenly shorter than he was.

She hadn't grown much, by the looks of it. The top of her head just skimmed his shoulder, and she was a woman now, not a girl. But it was still her. Still Hope Tabitha Barlow, who he'd sworn undying friendship to forever and ever all those years ago.

I wonder if she remembers that? He thought, a wry smile hovering at the corner of his mouth.

"Well, this is certainly a surprise. How many years, exactly, has it been since we last saw each other?"

"I dread to think." Hope said, laughing. "It's strange, but even though I recognized you immediately, you've changed so much. For the better, of course."

"I felt the same about you. Goodness, this feels surreal."

"It does, doesn't it?" Hope smiled self-consciously, small hands fluttering along the bodice of her gown, smoothing out her skirts. Ewan's smile faded as he took in what she was wearing. No jewels, no hint of perfume in the air. It was a plain brown dress with a starchy, old-fashioned lace collar at the neck. She looked beautiful in it – Hope had always been pretty, a fact which was returning to his attention in full force – but it was a plain, almost ugly dress. He could see neatly darned spots on the hem, and the cuffs had been turned down. He wanted, with an intensity that almost frightened him, to sweep her up in his arms and tell her that everything would be alright. That she was safe and happy here with him, and she wouldn't have to keep turning over the cuffs of her dresses like that, just to make them wearable.

Ewan realized, with a nasty, cold feeling, that things were not the same as they had been all those years ago. How old had he been when he last saw Hope? Eight? Nine? As soon as his father had become the next Duke of Darenwood, the family had whisked away to the country, and that was that. Then he'd met Caroline, and...

Caroline.

Ewan swayed a little on his feet. He felt sick.

Here he was, admiring Hope's beauty and reliving their happy times, when his wife lay dead in her grave, and had been for a full two years. He ought to be grieving, thinking of what he had lost. He hadn't thought of Caroline once since Hope stepped into the room, and that would not do.

He took a step back, suddenly eager to put distance between himself and Hope. Straightening up a little, Ewan cleared his throat, putting his hands behind his back.

Something bright faded away a little in Hope's expression. She'd always been intuitive, from what he remembered, and there was no mistaking the way she sagged a little where she stood, sensing his changing attitude.

"When did you become a governess?" Ewan asked, keen to dispel the uncomfortable atmosphere which had descended. Hope was still his friend, after all.

"It's a rather new development, actually." Hope answered, a light blush rising to her cheeks. "This... well, this will be my first position."

"Ah." Ewan thought briefly of Margaret, and how horrified she had been at the thought of a governess with no references, with this as her first position. He had better not mention this to her. "Well, no matter. I'm sure you have an excellent education. The agency spoke highly of you."

Hope nodded. "I've wanted a position for a long time, and I've been so excited... I can't believe it's you, Ewan! And you have a son, Lucas?"

Ewan smiled at that. "Yes, my little boy. He's a dear, I'm sure you'll like him."

"How old is he?"

"Only six. He is a very kind and thoughtful little boy. I know it's a cliched thing to say, but I'm tremendously proud of him. Hope, if you don't mind me asking, how did you come to be a governess? I haven't been in touch with your family for some time, but I haven't seen any of you around town."

Pain flashed across Hope's face, stark and vibrant, and Ewan wished he had not asked. It was too late, though. The words were out, and he could see Hope preparing herself to answer them.

"My father made some… mistakes." Hope managed. "Financial mistakes. There's no money, you see. No dowry for me, not a penny to live upon. Everything went to pay his debts, and now Papa is in debtor's prison."

"Good lord. I'm so sorry, Hope."

She shook her head. "It's fine, I have had time to come to terms with it. At the time, the humiliation was bad, but once I decided I would become a governess, that gave me purpose. I'm glad to be here. I've been living with my Aunt Ruth and my cousin, Agnes, and I've been happy, at least. Many people cannot say the same."

"Your aunt? What about your mother, Mrs Barlow?"

Another bad question. Hope swallowed reflexively, forcing a tiny, sad smile.

"My mother died some years ago."

"Oh. Oh, I am sorry, Hope." Ewan conjured up memories of a calm, relaxed woman with a languid smile, sprawled out on her elbows on a picnic basket, squinting against the sun. He'd always liked Mrs Barlow. She adored her little girl, her only child, and Hope adored her right back.

Hope cleared her throat, pushing back her shoulders, and Ewan sensed that she didn't want to discuss the matter further.

"This won't be strange, will it, Ewan? Me working as a governess in this house. After all, I didn't know that you would be my employer, and you didn't know that the agency would send me. Are you comfortable with all this?"

There was a spark of desperation in her eyes, and Ewan

realized that Hope very much wanted this position, and not just because she wanted an opportunity to see him again.

"Of course not." he said. "That is, I mean of course it won't be strange. I dare say you'll do a wonderful job. I might even feel more comfortable leaving my son with you than I did with the other governesses."

"Other governesses? The agency didn't mention any predecessors. If you don't mind me asking, what happened to the governesses before me?"

Before Ewan could stutter and stumble his way through an explanation, there was a sharp rap on the door. He caught a glimpse of Golightly, trying to enter and announce the new visitor, then Margaret pushed her way through into the room.

"Ah, the new governess. Good day to you, Miss Barlow." She waited, eyebrows raised, obviously expecting Hope to say something respectful and drop a curtsey.

"Mrs Darnell!" Hope gasped. "Oh, I remember you!"

That was the wrong thing to say, entirely the wrong thing. Anger darkened Margaret's brow, her lips pressing together in a tight, thin line. She glared at Hope, poised to say something.

"Mother, you remember Hope, don't you? Hope Barlow?" Ewan intervened quickly. "You and Mrs Barlow were very close at one time."

The anger did not dissipate. "I do not recall, Ewan, no. I worked hard to leave behind my vulgar acquaintances and unsuitable friends when I became the Duchess of Darenwood. Your father and I brought you to the country to get away from vulgarity, Ewan. I'm afraid I do not recall the Barlows at all."

She was lying. Ewan could have sworn she was lying. There was a flicker of recognition in his mother's eyes when he mentioned Hope's name. That didn't matter, though, if Margaret had chosen to forget her acquaintance with the Barlow family, there was very little he could do about it.

"Ah, I see." Ewan managed.

Hope had gone an interesting shade of red.

"Oh, I'm so sorry, I have offended you, Mrs... well, it won't be Mrs Darnell anymore, will it? Your Grace, I mean, of course. I am sorry."

Margaret's anger deflated a little, but her bristles were still up. Like an angry porcupine, or the hackles on a dog.

"Yes, well. This is not an auspicious start, Miss Barlow. I'm sure there was an acquaintanceship at one point – I shall not accuse you of making that up – but it is over now, and this is a professional relationship. My son has given me jurisdiction over the education of Master Lucas."

Ewan regretted that with all his heart.

But then, was it such a bad idea? At one time, Hope had sent his heart fluttering and beating madly. They were only children, but he remembered how butterflies would explode in his stomach when he saw her, the feeling that came when he met Caroline for the first time all those years later.

Ewan very much did not want those feelings to resurface. He was a widower, grieving his loss, and remarriage was not at all the thing for him. It complicated things.

Yes, it was certainly for the best that Margaret took charge of this business.

Hope glanced between him and Margaret, eyes wide. Understanding dawned slowly, then she swallowed hard, folded her hands in front of her waist, and pointed herself towards Margaret.

"I do beg your pardon, your Grace. I should very much like to start again, if you would permit it." Hope said, her voice subdued.

Ewan backed away to give the two women space but couldn't quite make himself turn around and look out of the window again.

Margaret quizzed Hope thoroughly, asking her various questions about dealing with children, her education, how she could go about teaching, how she would administer discipline, and so on.

"You seem educated enough." Margaret said grudgingly. "Very well, we shall introduce you to young Master Lucas tomorrow."

"Tomorrow?" Ewan spoke up. "I promised Lucas that he could meet her today."

Margaret pursed her lips. "Yes, well, now I think that tomorrow might be best. That will give Miss Barlow a chance to settle in and collect herself."

"Whatever you think is best, your Grace." Hope said, eyes

directed demurely downwards. Her gaze flicked up, darting over to Ewan. Their eyes met. Hope, obviously not expecting to be caught in a stare, flushed and hastily looked away. For some reason not entirely known to himself, Ewan felt himself reddening too.

He prayed that Margaret had not noticed.

Margaret eyed Hope for a long moment, eyes narrowed.

"You are younger than our previous governesses, Miss Barlow."

"That only means I have the youth and strength to go racing after Master Lucas, your Grace."

"Humph. You're prettier than a governess ought to be. I do hope that when we have male guests visiting, you won't make a fool of yourself and us by coquetting, or..."

"Mother!" Ewan interrupted, shocked. "There's no need for that."

"I'm happy to stay in my room when I am not taking care of Master Lucas." Hope said, her face carefully blank.

Margaret was not finished. She took a slow, methodical step forward.

"One thing I would like to make clear before you begin, Miss Barlow. I imagine that at one time, you and my son were on a relatively equal footing. Our families may even have been on an equal footing. Times have changed, and this is no longer the case. This may be a difficult truth to accept, but a household – and indeed, the world – runs smoothly only when everyone accepts their proper place. Do you understand?"

A blush was heating Hope's cheeks again. She was staring down at her shoes, but at the mention of her proper place, her gaze flicked up again, looking Margaret steadily in the eyes.

Don't let her see any defiance or anger, Ewan thought, with a pang of fear. She'll send you back.

He had backed himself into a corner. He had given his word that his mother would manage the governess, and now it was too late to take it back.

"Of course, I understand. I shall stay in my proper place at all times." Hope said, her voice clear and firm. "Your Grace."

Margaret did not seem pleased. She obviously sensed some insubordination but could not decide from where she sensed it.

"Hm. Well, I suppose you shall do. I'll show you the parts of the house you'll be using – the schoolroom and so on – and then you can retire to rest for a few hours."

Margaret turned on her heel, striding from the room. She gestured impatiently for Hope to follow her.

Hope glanced up at Ewan, and her expression was shuttered and unreadable.

"Good day, your Grace." She said, her voice neutral.

Chapter Seven

Mrs Darnell – no, Hope must remember not to call her that – the Dowager Duchess marched quickly along the hallways, heels ringing out on the cold, well-polished stone. She stayed a few paces ahead of Hope at all times and did not look back to check that she was being followed. She was a tall woman and did not bother to adjust her stride to allow Hope to keep up.

So, Hope puffed and panted along behind her, hating how loud her shoes sounded on the stone. Should she apologize for that? Or would speaking out of turn be a bad idea?

The decision was made for her.

"Once you are settled, Golightly will arrange to have your shoes taken to the cobblers." The Dowager said, her voice carrying easily in the cavernous hallway. "All members of our household wear felt pads on their soles, as to avoid vulgar noisiness."

Except for the Duke and the Dowager, of course. That went without saying. It was clearly just a rule for the servants, with whom Hope had just been categorized.

"I do apologize." Hope said breathlessly. "But wouldn't that make your shoes slippery?"

The Dowager did not grace this with a response. "I take it you have another pair of shoes?"

"Yes, but…"

"Then wear those starting tomorrow and leave your current ones outside your bedroom door. I'm not sure my nerves can take the constant clacking. Now, let me introduce you to the housekeeper. She will inform you of what to do with your laundry, meals, cleaning, etcetera, and I will deal with the rest of your duties later."

"Mrs Golightly?"

The Dowager stopped dead, so that Hope nearly walked into her back.

"I beg your pardon?"

Hope coloured. "The butler – Mr Golightly – told me. I think it's sweet that they are married, don't you think? They must be very happy."

"Hm. I see. Well, seeing as you are so well-informed, we

shall skip the visit to the kitchen and Mrs Golightly, and go straight to the schoolroom."

Hope bit her lip. The Dowager turned on her heel and marched away, at the same punishing pace as before. Hope followed, cursing herself. She'd made another mistake. Why couldn't she just hold her tongue?

It was too late now. She would have to find out what to do about meals and laundry later. For now, the Dowager was veering towards a huge, wide, red-carpeted staircase curving round and up to the first floor.

"Of course, it is preferable for you to take the servants' staircases." The Dowager said, beginning her ascent. "And the servants' passages, when necessary. However, as you'll be accompanying Lucas most of the time, that won't be practical. So, you can take the main halls and stairs if you wish. However, in your free time, or if Lucas is not around, you may wish to consider taking more appropriate routes around the house for a person of your station. Is this understood?"

"Yes, your Grace."

Hope hated how subdued and miserable her own voice sounded. The Dowager's voice, droning on and on about Rules and Expectations faded into the background.

She kept seeing Ewan, the way the delight on his face had dropped away so quickly, and how he'd stiffened up, moving back from her. He hadn't even bothered to intervene when the Dowager was humiliating her so thoroughly, going on about her proper place, and essentially telling her not to flirt with male guests.

How embarrassing.

Hope did not remember the Dowager very well from her childhood. She had a vague, fuzzy memory of an anxious woman with a shrill voice, who had often sat in the park beside her mother. She remembered her mother sending a long, rambling letter, full of crossings-out and little drawings, addressed to the Duchess of something-or-other. She'd written a letter to the mystery duchess several times, but never received a reply. The letters stopped, of course, and Mrs Barlow seemed sad for a while. But it never lasted long, and Hope was too young to understand the nuances of friendship and loss, anyway. Unbeknownst to Hope, her father was already beginning to fritter away their fortune, so the fates of the Barlows and the Darnells were drawing further and further apart.

And now here she was, little more than a servant in the home of a woman who had once been her mother's friend.

Not that the Dowager was admitting that, of course. No doubt she'd erased Mrs Barlow from her life and her mind when she became a duchess.

A flash of resentment went through Hope, but she took a deep breath and forced through it.

She needed this position. Desperately. And if that meant dancing around the haughty Dowager Duchess, then she would do that.

They went through twisting hallways, all decorated with the same expensive, patterned wallpaper and thick pile red carpet, until Hope gave up any idea of ever finding her way out again.

"Here is the schoolroom." The Dowager said shortly, stopping before a door and pushing it open. "Go in. Take in the space."

It wasn't a suggestion, so Hope did so, stepping inside and looking around.

It was a large, high-ceilinged room, a little cold, with an unlit grate at the back of the room. Bookcases lined the walls, packed with various books. There were two desks in the room, facing each other. The larger of the two – which Hope took to be hers – had a large blackboard on the wall behind it. A globe sat on the desk, as well as a small box of supplies. Paper, pens, ink, pencils, and so on.

"I'm sure you'll find the schoolroom appropriately stocked." The Dowager said, as if daring Hope to contradict her. "Inside your desk, you'll find some of Miss Mullins' notes on Master Lucas' current education. That way, you can pick up exactly where she left off. I will occasionally sit in for the lessons, and you will not be given notice of that. I may drop in at any time and demand a summary of what you've been doing that day, or that week. Is that understood?"

Hope swallowed hard, trying to will away the feeling of dread in the pit of her stomach.

"I understand, your Grace."

"Once you've proven yourself to be a trustworthy and

competent governess, you will be left more to your own devices, but for now, assume that I am always watching. Always. Do you understand?"

"I do."

The Dowager narrowed her eyes, taking a step closer.

"You were not my choice, Miss Barlow. You are too young, with too little experience. This… this connection you claim to have with our family does not work in your favour. Quite the reverse, actually. However, my son has decided that you will stay, and it is now up to you to prove yourself to me. I have high, exacting standards, and time shall tell whether you can meet them or not."

Hope swallowed hard, lifting her chin. "Thank you for your honesty, your Grace."

The Dowager hadn't been expecting that. She blinked, annoyance clouding her face as she realized Hope had stayed calm and composed.

"I am here as a governess, your Grace." Hope pressed on. "No more, no less. I am not a servant. I will have the care of Master Lucas, and that will be my sole and all-encompassing task. Rest assured that I will treat that task with the seriousness it deserves."

The two women stared at each other for a long, tense moment.

The tension was broken by a woman bustling along the hallway, humming to herself and flicking a feather duster around.

She stopped dead when she saw the Dowager.

"Oh, your Grace!" she gasped. "I didn't know… I thought nobody was in here. I was just going to dust the schoolroom. I…"

"Never mind, Emily." The Dowager said briskly. "You may take the new governess to her room. I shall see you tomorrow, Miss Barlow. Breakfast is served at eight. Lessons begin at nine, but I shall expect to see you in the school at quarter to nine. Sharp."

She didn't wait for a response. Turning on her heel, the Dowager strode away down the halls, and was soon out of sight.

Hope let out a breath she hadn't even realized that she was holding.

A round-faced young woman peered into the schoolroom.

"Oh. Hello, miss. You're the new governess, then. I'm Emily."

Emily was a stocky young woman with dark hair tucked under a mob cap, and a profusion of freckles. She smiled shyly at

Hope, who almost sagged in relief at the sight of a friendly face.

"Yes, hello. It's nice to meet you. My name is Hope Barlow. Her Grace was just... just showing me the schoolroom."

Emily wrinkled her nose. "It's dark and cold in there. I hate it, and so does young Master Lucas. I'm his nursemaid, you see. Come along, I'll show you to your room."

Obviously having decided that Hope was an ally, Emily flashed her a mischievous smile and scuttled back along the hallway. Hurriedly closing the door behind her, Hope scurried after her.

She thought about making a comment about how the Dowager did not seem to like her but decided against it. It wasn't a good idea to start off her first day in her new position by complaining about her employer.

"There have been other governesses, then?" Hope asked.

"Oh, yes, lots. Her Grace, the Dowager, is very picky, so they come and go. But I'm sure you'll do fine." Emily added hastily, smiling apologetically.

There was a low, blue-painted door just a hallway's length away from the schoolroom. Emily stopped in front of the door and pushed it open.

"This is your room. It's been aired out and the sheets changed."

Hope stepped inside, taking in the room that was to be her new home. She saw that her bags had been brought her, dumped unceremoniously in the middle of the floor.

She'd hoped for something a little larger, so that half of the room could be a parlour and half a bedroom, but no such luck. A single bed was pushed into the corner, laid with plenty of blankets and quilts. There was a nightstand with a single, half-melted candle, a washbasin in the corner with a chipped porcelain bowl, a smeared mirror hanging above, and a trunk at the bottom of the bed for clothes. Aside from that, there was a threadbare armchair beside the cold, empty hearth, and that was all.

There wasn't even a rug on the floor.

"Oh, this is nice." Hope said lamely. "Thank you."

Emily chuckled. "I know it's not nice. Miss Mullins, the last governess, said that it wasn't a patch on her old place. She had two rooms there, a bedroom and a parlour. It sounded ever so nice."

"Then why did she leave?"

Emily shrugged. "The boys she was taking care of grew up and went to boarding school, so they didn't need her anymore. That's what happens when you're a governess. You've got to save up, so that when you're too old to hop around looking for jobs, you've got something to fall back on."

Fear clawed at Hope's throat, stark and worrying. Of course, governesses were never permanent members of a household. Even a maid could stay in the same house her whole life, gradually clawing her way up to be the housekeeper one day. But a governess had nowhere else to go once the children didn't need her anymore.

"Sorry, I didn't mean to worry you." Emily said, apologetically. "When are you meeting young Master Lucas? He's very sweet."

"People keep saying that. The Dowager said that I can meet him tomorrow."

"Oh. That's a pity. Still, I suppose you need some time to rest, eh?"

"What... what about food?" Hope asked, blushing. She didn't want to tell Emily how her misstep had led to the Dowager omitting the introduction to Mrs Golightly. "And I was told that my shoes needed felt soles, so it's not so noisy when I walk around."

Emily shot her a pitying glance. "Yes, we all have that. It's very slippery, I can tell you. Watch your step on the servants' stairs, by the way. As to dinner, I'll have a tray sent up for you."

That was something, at least. Hope was a little embarrassed to admit how hungry she was feeling.

"Shouldn't I eat dinner in the servants' hall with the rest of you?"

Emily shrugged. "I don't know. I don't think so. None of the other governesses did. Miss Mullins ate up here, and so did all the others. I can't quite recall their names, now."

"I see. Well, thank you, Emily. You've been very kind. It's a lot to take in, and this place is like a maze. I can't fathom how I'll ever learn to find my way around."

Emily chuckled at that, smiling more widely. "Oh, you'll get used to it, Miss Barlow. We all did. Of course, you're in the family's part of the house, rather than the servants' quarters. That part is ours, you see. Well, I really must get going. It was nice to meet you, and I'll see about that dinner tray as soon as possible."

"Yes, thank you." Hope said mechanically. Emily withdrew, closing the door after her, leaving Hope alone.

She sat down slowly on the edge of her bed.

Home sweet home, she thought bitterly.

Chapter Eight

"You're late," Margaret said irritably.

Ewan smothered a sigh, sliding into a seat at the dining table. "Sorry, Mother. Where is Hope?"

"If you are talking about Miss Barlow, she is in her room." Margaret shot a Look at Ewan over the rim of her wine glass. "I hope you're not suggesting that we should welcome a governess at our dining table, Ewan?"

Ewan bit his lip. "No, of course not. But she was our friend once, and I thought you might want to catch up."

"I don't know why you would think that." Margaret said acidly, replacing her wine glass with a clack. "She's a governess, Ewan. No good ever came from mixing stations and allowing people to step out of their proper place. I don't want you to encourage her."

"Of course I won't." Ewan answered automatically, not bothering to ask what encouraging her might entail.

They ate in silence, only the sound of clinking cutlery breaking the silence. Ewan found his thoughts almost entirely occupied by Hope, and the Barlows in general.

So much had happened since he and Hope had promised to be friends forever, all those years ago. He'd never have imagined, not even for an instant, that he would one day be a duke of anything. But now, this was his life, and they might as well have been strangers.

There'd been Caroline, and then Lucas had been born. Ewan closed his eyes momentarily, not wanting to relive that miserable time when he realized that he would lose his wife, and be left to raise Lucas alone.

"I wonder what happened?" Ewan said aloud, earning himself a sharp stare from his mother.

"What did you say?"

"I said that I wonder what happened to the Barlows? After all, Hope's father was a viscount, wasn't he? Hope should have married someone suitable by now, but instead she's a governess? It seems strange."

Margaret pursed her lips together. "Lots of young women

pass up on perfectly good opportunities to be married and settled, out of perversity and childishness. I dare say Miss Barlow chose to reject whatever offers came her way, filling her head with nonsense about love and romance instead, and now she has cause to regret it. Or perhaps she simply didn't receive many offers, if any. She is a plain little thing, don't you think?"

"Plain?" Ewan echoed, conjuring up an image of Hope's large blue eyes, delicately featured face, and blonde curls. "Oh, Mother, you can't possibly say that Hope is plain. She's exceptionally pretty."

"That won't do her any favours as a governess." Margaret snapped. "And for heaven's sake, Ewan, please call her Miss Barlow. We are not on first name terms with her."

"Why not? We call Emily by her first name, after all, and she is Lucas' nursemaid."

Margaret sniffed. "Yes, well, Miss Barlow made it abundantly clear that she is not a servant. She has chosen to live in limbo, and I am more than happy to oblige."

Ewan said nothing, smothering a smile. He could imagine Hope speaking firmly but politely to his mother, telling her that she wasn't a servant and wouldn't be treated as such.

Margaret was right, though – that wouldn't have done her any favours, anymore than being a pretty governess. She'd be safe in this household, of course, but in other households, pretty women might risk harassment.

That wasn't a pleasant thought. Ewan shifted in his seat, conscious of a feeling of anger at the idea of Hope being harassed by some drunken, lecherous fool who'd hired her to teach his children.

He cleared his throat, glancing up to find his mother's eyes on him.

"Of course, Mother," he said placidly. "Miss Barlow it is, of course."

"Remember, I will be handling her tutorage of Lucas." Margaret said pointedly. "We agreed on that, did we not?"

"Of course we did. I have no objections to that."

Margaret sniffed, as if she didn't quite believe him. They continued with their dinner, another awkward silence springing up between them.

Once again, Ewan found himself thinking about Hope. He imagined her sitting up in that cold, comfortless room beside the schoolroom. He knew what the room looked like, of course, and found himself wishing that they'd made the place a little more homely. A rug or two on the floor, for example, or a few extra candles.

It was too late now, of course. He would speak privately to Mrs Golightly and ask her to spruce up Hope's room while she was out.

Miss Barlow's room, he meant.

"You seem very lost in thought, Ewan. Is everything alright? I do hope the arrival of Miss Barlow hasn't shaken you. I can't blame you. I wouldn't like to think of an old acquaintance tutoring my children or working in my house." Margaret remarked. "Those old connections open the way to all sorts of proprieties. Servants need to know what their place is, and they must be taught to stay in it. It's harder to keep those boundaries firm and clear if one is dealing with an old friend. I shouldn't blame you for wanting her gone, my dear."

Ewan cleared his throat, squaring his shoulders. "Not at all, Mother. I'm just thinking about... about other things, that's all. I'm sure that Miss Barlow is completely capable."

"We disagree on that, but only time will tell." Margaret remarked.

"Oh, I forgot to mention," Ewan said, suddenly keen to change the subject, "Robert is back in town."

"Oh, Lord Ashbury? How wonderful." Margaret said, sounding as if she thought it anything but.

Lord Ashbury was a good friend of Ewan's. They had become friends years ago, but not before Ewan and his family had taken up their dukedom and their lives had changed. He wasn't as old a friend as Hope – Miss Barlow – but he was still a good one.

"We'll meet up at the club later tomorrow." Ewan said, pushing away his plate. "It'll be good to catch up."

And it would get him out of the house while poor Hope Barlow started on her first day as a governess.

I hope she really is good at teaching children, Ewan thought wryly, *since I've taken quite a chance on her. If this is a disaster, I suppose I'll have to let Mother choose the next one.*

He glanced up, feeling eyes on him, and once again caught his mother staring at him shrewdly across the table.

"You certainly are preoccupied tonight." Margaret stated. "I shan't press you for an explanation, but I shall draw my own conclusions. Will you be dining here tomorrow night, or out at your club with Lord Ashbury?"

Ewan stretched, getting to his feet with a smile.

"I haven't decided yet. I'll send you a note from the club, either way."

"Hm. And where exactly are you going?"

"To bed, Mother. I'm exhausted. If I go to the drawing room, there's a good chance I'll simply fall asleep on the sofa with a book in my hands."

Ewan moved around the table to press a kiss to his mother's powdery cheek and headed out towards the stairs. Something made him pause at the foot of the stairs. He glanced back, catching his mother's eye through the open dining room door. She was eyeing him with a strange expression in her eyes.

The expression was wiped away as soon as their eyes met, and Margaret flashed a quick smile instead.

Chapter Nine

Margaret kept an eye on the clock in the parlour, diligently ticking away. She knew that Miss Barlow was up, taking breakfast in her room. She should be down soon.

That was a little disappointing. Margaret had hoped that the girl would be late. Ewan likely wouldn't stand for her being dismissed for lateness on her first day, but it was certainly a black mark against her.

The clock ticked steadily towards half-past eight. Miss Barlow was instructed to come here for half-past eight exactly, to confer with Margaret and meet Lucas for the first time.

Margaret had used the time to read the letter hanging loosely from her hand. The Emsworths were back in town, which was exciting. Lady Harriet Emsworth, Margaret's friend, would want to come and visit. Her daughter, Viola, was not yet married. In her letter, Lady Harriet bemoaned the fact, and seemed entirely at a loss as to why her daughter was not yet married. After all, she pointed out, she was exceptionally beautiful, well-bred, rich, and charming.

Margaret agreed with all of those points except for the 'charming' part. If she had to choose one word to describe Miss Viola Emsworth, it would be 'spoilt'.

However, she was beautiful, and that was really the only quality a lady needed in the marriage mart, so long as she had a decent fortune and knew how to act.

Unfortunately, that meant that Miss Barlow was even more of a threat. Margaret pressed her lips together, leaning back in her seat. She'd hoped for an older woman, or at least a plain woman. Miss Mullins had been perfectly plain, and Margaret had never even considered the danger of an improper match between her and Ewan. But now that Miss Barlow was here, Ewan's old friend...

Margaret swallowed back her fear. Ewan was to marry sooner or later; she knew that. Caroline had always said that he should, that she wanted him to be happy and not lonely. However, Margaret had assumed that she would have control of that. A sweet, pliable, suitable young woman wouldn't object to Margaret staying here and helping her to run the household.

The plain truth was that Margaret liked living here. She only had one child, and not much else in her life to concern herself. The Dower House on the estate loomed, a quiet, dull little place designed for a widow to live out her days in obscurity. She hadn't lived there for years, and only for the first year of Caroline and Ewan's marriage. Once they learned that Caroline was expecting a baby, she was invited to come and stay with them, and simply didn't leave.

Margaret shivered at the thought of returning to the Dower House. That wasn't home. It had never felt like home. It was far away from London, with nothing in the way of entertainment or company.

I can't go back, she thought wildly. I won't. She'd loved being the Duchess. The position had suited her down to the ground. It had entailed some sacrifices, of course. A Duchess could not keep on the low friends she'd kept before. More was expected of her, but Margaret flattered herself on rising to the challenge.

As the Dowager Duchess, mother to an an unmarried Duke, Margaret was still the Duchess, more or less. But if Ewan married, that would all change.

So it had better be the right woman, Margaret thought, with a flash of frustration. She wasn't a fool. Ewan was lonely, anyone with eyes could see that. Margaret had no objection to his marrying again, but it had to be to the proper woman.

She glanced down at Lady Harriet's letter again, and inspiration hit.

Rising quickly, Margaret hurried over to her writing desk.

My Dearest Harriet, she began, not caring about her handwriting,

I am shocked to hear that you are staying in a hotel! Of course, the London hotels in that area are particularly fine. Have I not told you the importance of keeping a house in London? Still, that is of no matter.

I must insist that you come and stay here with us. I have not seen you in an age, my dear friend, and I would very much enjoy your company. Bring sweet Viola, of course.

I am shocked and upset to hear that Viola has not yet found a match. It seems that Society has no taste these days, and proper young ladies are being entirely ignored. But enough of that – you and I can set the world to rights once you have arrived.

My son, the Duke, is here of course. Is Viola fond of children? I daresay she is – she is such a sweet girl. My grandson is also here, and I suppose Viola will dote on him! As you know, my son is widowed, and tremendously lonely these days. It is a hard thing for a mother to accept. Of course, you know this, since your poor Viola had not yet found a suitable man.

However, I believe that these things have a way of working out. So, write back to me as soon as you can – I shall eagerly await your reply, and your company.

Your Dear Friend,
Margaret Darnell, Dowager Duchess of Darenwood

Margaret leaned back with a satisfied sigh, running her eyes over the note. Hopefully her hint would be taken. If not, she could always talk to Harriet when she arrived.

Viola and Ewan would suit very well. They were both rich, and both extremely handsome. Harriet might balk at the idea that Viola's children would not inherit the dukedom, but that couldn't be helped. Viola ought to have secured a man earlier in the Season, then.

Margaret hastily folded up the paper, sealing it with a knot of wax. As she did so, there was a light tap on the door, and Mrs Golightly entered.

"What is it?" Margaret asked, not looking up.

"Miss Barlow is here, your Grace," Mrs Golightly said. "Shall I show her in?"

Margaret heaved a sigh, and immediately wished she hadn't. The housekeeper was far too well-bred and clever to indicate that she'd heard, but Margaret knew she had. She didn't want the whole household to know that she disliked the governess. It was beneath her.

She glanced sharply at Mrs Golightly, whose round face was as bland and impassive as always. Margaret considered saying something but decided against it. It would only make matters worse.

"Have this delivered immediately," Margaret said, holding out the note. "And wait for a response. It's a matter of urgency."

"Of course, your Grace." Mrs Golightly said, crossing the room to take the note.

Margaret returned to her seat, taking her time to get herself settled. She sat upright, back straight, posture perfect, and shook out her skirts a little. She glanced at the clock. Exactly half past eight. If she delayed a little bit, it would be later than that, and then she could claim that Miss Barlow was late.

No, that was too petty.

Margaret sighed. "Show the governess in, then."

Chapter Ten

Composing herself and pasting a polite yet subservient (she hoped) smile on her face, Hope stepped forward into the parlour.

The Dowager sat in state on an overstuffed sofa, positioned carefully in the centre of the room so that it was the first thing a person's eyes landed on when they first entered. She was resplendent in black satin, lace, and ropes upon ropes of pearls.

It all seemed a bit much for so early in the morning – breakfast was barely over – but Hope was careful not to let a hint of this show on her face. She made a neat curtsey, keeping the smile on her face.

"Good morning to you, your Grace. I hope you slept well."

The Dowager sniffed, not bothering to return the comment. "I take it you have breakfasted?"

"I have, your Grace."

"Good. Then we can begin immediately. Emily is bringing Master Lucas to meet us here. Now, I will not be overseeing your lessons today, as I have important guests whose arrival I must prepare for. I do hope you won't take advantage of my absence."

That comment stung, as it was undoubtedly intended to, but Hope kept a serene smile on her face.

"Of course not, your Grace. I am very much looking forward to meeting Master Lucas."

Hope shifted her weight from foot to foot, hoping that the Dowager would invite her to sit down. Hope had eaten her breakfast in a rush, panicking in case she would be late for her first day of work. In the end, her tea hadn't cooled down enough for her to drink it, so she was forced to leave it sitting on a table in her room. A cup of tea sounded delicious, but somehow Hope doubted that the Dowager would think to offer tea to the governess.

"I have a very high expectation of you, Miss Barlow." The Dowager finally spoke again. "I do hope you won't disappoint."

Hope inclined her head. "I am looking forward very much to the challenge, your Grace. I hope I won't let you down, either. Is there anything else I should know before I start work? A particular subject you would like me to deal with first, or a particular teaching method that Master Luke responds well to?"

The Dowager blinked, as if taken aback.

"I can't think of anything." She replied shortly, giving Hope a quick, sharp look of dislike, as if resenting her for the question.

Before the silence could get too awkward, there was a tap on the door, and Emily entered, leading a small boy by the hand.

Master Lucas was small for his age, with large brown eyes that dominated his oval-shaped, pale face. He had brown hair, and an attempt had been made to flatten down his curls with water.

It had not succeeded.

He was clutching Emily's hands and did not smile.

"Miss Barlow, this is Master Lucas Darnell." The Dowager said grandly. "He is the son of the Duke of Darenwood and will one day hold the title of the Duke of Darenwood himself. Treat him with the according respect."

Emily glanced between them, eyes wide, and poor Lucas shrank back at his grandmother's sharp tone. Hope gritted her teeth and dropped into a neat curtsey.

"Master Lucas, it's a pleasure to meet you. I hope we'll be friends."

Lucas said nothing. He stared at Hope with large, wide eyes, and did not smile. Hope's heart sank a little. She'd hoped he would be a chatty, effusive child, easy to talk to and easy to teach. This quiet, serious little boy would pose a challenge.

Silence descended, which Hope broke by clearing her throat and smiling brightly at the Dowager.

"May I take Master Lucas up to the schoolroom and begin his lessons? Emily can accompany us, if you like."

The Dowager shrugged. "As you please, Miss Barlow. I shall expect a full account of today's events from you before dinner, and I shall require such information every day for the rest of the week. After that, we shall see."

Hope curtsied and said nothing.

***

Hope and Lucas walked side by side down the corridor, with Emily following behind. Hope made one or two attempts to draw the little boy into conversation, but he replied with quiet, one-word answers. She was just resigning herself to a few long hours of painful silence when Lucas finally spoke.

"Where did Miss Mullins go?"

Hope swallowed hard. "I don't exactly know, I'm afraid. I daresay she found another position."

Lucas didn't seem reassured by this. "I liked Miss Mullins."

"From what I hear, Miss Mullins liked you too. Very much so."

"Then why did she leave?"

That was a very good question, and Hope did not have a good answer.

"I hope we'll be friends, you and I." she said, glancing down at the small boy and smiling.

"Yes, you said that." Lucas had his gaze fixed on his feet. "Grandmama doesn't seem to like you."

Hope winced. Behind her, she heard Emily smother a giggle.

"No," Hope said slowly, "but that is because she's very fond of you and wants to be sure that I'm going to teach you correctly and take care of you. Once she knows that I will, I daresay we'll be good friends, too."

Hope didn't believe that, of course, but Lucas seemed convinced, at least.

They arrived at the schoolroom, and Hope was relieved to see that a fine fire had been set up in the grate. At least they wouldn't freeze today.

Lucas moved straight over to a desk and sat down, placing his hands palms down on the wood desk in front of him. He stared seriously at Hope, feet swinging inches above the ground.

"I suppose we shall have to do Algebra." He said with resignation.

Hope perched on the edge of her own desk. "Do you want to do Algebra?"

This question seemed to surprise Lucas. "No, but Grandmama said..."

"You can learn Algebra when you are a little older. I suppose there'll be lots of opportunities. Today, though, I want to learn about you, Lucas. What subjects you like, which subjects you find difficult, and so on. So, what sort of things do you like doing?"

Lucas shifted in his seat, some of the seriousness leaving his small face.

"I like to play outside, but only if it is dry and fine. I don't like being muddy."

"We have that in common, I think." Hope said and was rewarded with a tiny smile.

"Yes, and I have to scrub out his clothes when they're all muddy!" Emily remarked, and Lucas' smile widened just the smallest bit.

"What do you like to do when it's rainy outside, then?" Hope pressed.

"I like to read books." Lucas said, clearly warming to his theme. "I can't read words with very long words just yet. Grandmama says that I should read improving books, but they never have any pictures, and they're ever so dull. I like books of stories."

"Can I tell you a secret, Master Lucas?" Hope said, leaning forward with a smile. "It's a very shocking thing to hear from a governess."

She had him hooked now. Lucas leaned forward, engrossed.

"What is it, Miss Barlow?"

"I prefer storybooks to improving books," Hope admitted. "Shocking, isn't it?"

He gave a tiny giggle. "We've got lots of storybooks."

"I can't wait to read them. Now, have you ever tried writing your own stories, Lucas?"

Lucas shook his head.

"I see. Well, for our first lesson, why don't you try and write your own story? We'll spend half an hour writing our own stories – Emily can join in too – and at the end of the half an hour, we'll read over them, and see what we think. What do you say?"

"I like that idea!" Lucas said, visibly perking up.

"I'm glad someone does." Emily grumbled, looking around her for a piece of paper.

Chapter Eleven

Ewan stared down at the pile of work waiting for him on his desk. He made no move to start on it.

His study was quiet at this time of day, sun filtering in through the half-drawn curtains, the air still and peaceful.

And yet he couldn't seem to collect his thoughts.

Had Hope met Lucas yet? What did they think of each other?

I wish I hadn't been so unkind to her when she first arrived.

Ewan closed his eyes. He wished he could have that time over, and act differently during their first meeting. Hope was his old friend, and yet he turned a cold shoulder towards her. No doubt she already felt strange, as the daughter of a viscount, having to seek work as a governess. An old friend acting like a stranger would only have made the situation ten times worse.

And then Margaret had been so unkind to her, so overbearing and haughty. Poor Hope, thinking that she'd found a lifeline, a proper position for herself, only to realize that she would get nothing but slights and injustices while she was here. It wasn't fair.

Outside in the hallway, Ewan heard the rhythmic clack-clack-clack of approaching footsteps. That could only be his mother – all the rest of the household were made to wear felted soles to make their footsteps quiet.

Sure enough, Margaret opened the door without warning and stepped in. Ewan swallowed his annoyance.

"I wish you'd knock, Mother." He said lightly. It wasn't worth the battle of insisting, though.

Margaret didn't bother to respond, instead dropping heavily into the seat opposite Ewan's desk, not waiting to be asked.

"I have some news, Ewan."

"Is it about Miss Barlow? How is her first day going? Does Lucas like her?"

Margaret gave a little moue of annoyance. "I haven't been able to check on the girl yet. I asked Emily an hour ago, when they stopped for tea, and she said that the girl seemed to be competent enough. I shall be the judge of that, of course. No, this is nothing to do with the governess. This is good news, very exciting."

Ewan doubted that very much. He leaned back in his seat, raising an eyebrow.

"Well? What is it, then?"

Margaret beamed. "Lady Harriet Emsworth and Miss Viola Emsworth are coming to stay."

Ewan missed a beat. "And that is supposed to be good news, is it?"

Margaret's smile faded. "Why, are you not happy? They're back in town, and staying in a hotel, of all places. I told Harriet a dozen times if I told her once, she must have a place in town. I remember one time I said..."

She trailed off into an anecdote, and Ewan stopped listening.

He knew Lady Emsworth and Miss Emsworth, of course. Lady Harriet, as she was affectionately called by her friends, was a corpulent woman with a false front and a false smile. She appeared to be a jovial, friendly, good-tempered woman, but in fact adored gossip, the more malicious, the better. If there was no juicy gossip for her to hear, she would make it up. She had started rumours that had ruined not one, not two, but three separate young debutantes. She'd been eyeing Ewan with a calculating eye recently, and he had no illusions as to why.

The reason why, of course, was Miss Emsworth – Viola. Viola was a very fashionable and beautiful young lady, with glossy black hair and flashing blue eyes – it was very important that a lady's eyes flashed, for some reason – and a perfectly moulded face and form. She had been immensely popular among the young gentlemen during her first Season, but her popularity started to wear off towards the end. Ewan guessed that she had recently finished her second Season and was willing to bet that she had no fiancé on the horizon.

"Ewan? Are you listening to me?"

Ewan flushed, turning his attention back to his mother.

"I'm sorry, Mother, I was daydreaming. What were you saying?"

Margaret heaved a sigh. "I was saying, Ewan, that we really do owe it to Lady Harriet to offer them accommodation. She is a great friend of mine, and I would love to see her. Besides, I already sent off the note."

Ewan bit his lip. No doubt the note had been sent off before she asked his permission for this very reason – he could hardly kick up a fuss once the invitation had been extended.

"Do you think they'll accept?" he asked.

Margaret hid a tiny smile. "I am sure of it."

Perhaps this would be a good thing. After all, with her friend staying in the house, Margaret might worry less about the new governess and simply enjoy spending time with Lady Harriet.

"Very well, Mother. I do wish you'd asked, but I suppose we can't let poor Lady Harriet stay in a hotel."

"And Miss Emsworth." Margaret added, quick as lightning. "You can't forget about her."

Ewan grimaced, conjuring up memories of a self-obsessed, vain, and opinionated young woman. "I don't think there's much chance of that, Mother. No chance at all."

***

"Is he asleep?" Ewan whispered.

Emily was just coming out of Lucas' room, in the process of easing the door closed. She glanced back into the darkened room.

"He's just dropping off, your Grace. If you want to say goodnight to him, you can go in now."

Ewan nodded and smiled his thanks, slipping into Lucas' bedroom.

"Papa?" Lucas said sleepily, propping himself up on his elbow.

"Go to sleep, darling." Ewan murmured, perching on the edge of his son's bed. "I just came to say goodnight. Did you have a good day today? I'm sorry I didn't have much chance to see you. I was working all day in my study, you see."

Lucas pouted. "You're always working."

Ewan flinched at that. Lucas rarely said such things, and perhaps it had something to do with the fact he was so tired. He was right, though. Ewan was guiltily aware that he'd spent all day in his study, working diligently, trying not to think about Miss Barlow, Caroline, or wretched Viola Emsworth.

"I'm sorry, Lucas. I promise we'll do something fun together soon. Did you like Miss Barlow?"

Lucas' expression brightened. "Yes, she was a very nice lady.

She didn't make me do any Algebra."

Ewan smothered a smile. "I'm glad, but don't tell your grandmama that. She'll be shocked."

Lucas giggled. "She says that she likes storybooks too. She even let me write my own story. She said that it was very good and saved it to show you later."

"Well, I can't wait to read it. What else did you do?"

"We did boring things, like Arithmetic and Geography, because Miss Barlow says that they're important things to know about. I like her very much, Papa."

"That's good." Ewan said, smoothing back Lucas' hair from his forehead and leaning close to press a kiss to his forehead. "I'm glad to hear that."

"Papa..."

"Hm?"

"Is Miss Barlow going to leave like Miss Mullins did? I don't want her to go."

That question made Ewan feel cold and guilty. He leaned back, looking at Lucas' small, earnest face.

"I hope not." Ewan said carefully. "But if she decides to leave, I can't stop her, you know."

"I know." Lucas said, picking at the blankets. "Don't let Grandmama send her way, though."

Ewan swallowed hard. "I'll do my best, Lucas. Sleep tight, dearest."

Chapter Twelve

Two Days Later

"No, no, Lucas, there's a silent letter at the beginning. Like 'know', K-N-O-W, remember? Try again."

"K-N-O-W-L-E-D-G-E." Lucas spelled out, sounding his way through the long word with difficulty.

"That's exactly right." Hope said, beaming. "Well done, Lucas. Well done."

He grinned widely at the praise, writing the words down in his exercise book.

"Now, let's move on to..." Hope paused abruptly, ears pricking up at the sound of approaching footsteps. She was learning to hear the muffled, almost unnoticeable sound of the servants' footsteps, but the footsteps of the Dowager were always noticeable. The heels of her shoes rang out, heralding her arrival everywhere she went.

She spent a lot of time in the schoolroom, much to Hope's dismay. She popped in and out whenever she pleased, disrupting the flow of lessons, making suggestions and comments, and sometimes even suggesting an entire change of topic.

It was exhausting, and Hope had already learnt to dread the clacking sound of approaching footsteps.

Still, she pasted a smile on her face and turned towards the door in time for it to open.

"Good morning, your Gr..." Hope began, only to trail off.

It wasn't the Dowager.

"Papa!" Lucas exclaimed delightedly. "We're doing spelling. I learnt a new word. Knowledge: K-N-O-W-L-E-D-G-E. Knowledge."

"Very well done, Lucas! Good morning, Miss Barlow. I hope I'm not interrupting." Ewan said, smiling.

No, not Ewan. Hope had to remember that. His Grace, the Duke.

She hastily got to her feet and bobbed a curtsey.

"Not at all," she said lightly. "How can I help you, your Grace? Do you wish to sit on a lesson?"

"No, thank you. I think Lucas' grandmama is doing enough of

that. Can I have a moment to talk to Lucas?"

Hope suppressed a smile. Why on earth was he asking her permission? It wasn't as if she would deny him. Still, it felt good to be asked.

"Of course, your Grace. Shall I ring for tea?"

"If you like."

Ewan crouched down beside Lucas' desk, smiling up at him.

"Remember how I promised we would do something fun soon?"

Lucas' face lit up with excitement. It was obvious that he adored his father, and that warmed Hope's heart to see.

"Yes, yes! I remember! What are we going to do?"

"I thought I would ask you that. Tomorrow, I thought you could take a holiday – with Miss Barlow's permission, of course – and we could do something you want to do."

Lucas was practically vibrating with excitement.

"The Tower of London! Oh, and the Royal Menagerie!"

Ewan grinned. "Sounds exciting. What do you say, Miss Barlow? Do we have your permission?"

"Of course," she said, laughing. "Perhaps the day after, Lucas could write up a report on his day out, and that way we could turn it into something educational."

"Excellent! There you are, you see, Lucas! We're going to have a tremendous day together, you and me."

Lucas flung his arms around his father's broad shoulders, tipping himself out of his seat. Ewan caught him, laughing, holding him tight.

A lump formed in Hope's throat, and she turned away. Seeing Ewan with his son, so happy and domestic, made her feel... strange. That was the best word for it.

He is a duke, she reminded herself firmly. A duke, and your employer. He isn't little Ewan. Not anymore.

"You said you and me, Papa," Lucas said, pulling back. "You and me and Miss Barlow, you mean."

Hope winced, glancing back at them. Ewan half opened his mouth, meeting her eye.

"Ah..."

"I think your Papa wanted it to be just you and him, Master Lucas." Hope said lightly. "Won't that be fun?"

To her surprise, Lucas pouted.

"Can't Miss Barlow come too, Papa?"

Ewan didn't hesitate. "Of course she can, Lucas! What say you, Miss Barlow? Do you fancy seeing the Tower of London, and the Royal Menagerie? I'll buy you an ice."

"I... I don't want to intrude."

Ewan met her gaze, and his smile softened, just a little.

"You won't be intruding, I promise. I'd like you to be there, and Lucas certainly wants you to be there."

Hope felt herself blushing and forced a smile. It did sound wonderful. If only she wasn't going as a governess.

"I should love it. Thank you, your Grace."

"Hooray!" Lucas cheered.

"Now, let's talk about our plans. I think we ought to take the carriage down, and then... oh, what is it, Golightly?"

Hope flinched, glancing over her shoulder to see the butler standing unobtrusively in the doorway. As always, he'd crept up on velvet feet.

"Your Grace," Mr Golightly said, his voice as serene and unimposing as his manner, "Her Grace the Dowager Duchess requests your presence in the Green Parlour. Lady Emsworth and Miss Emsworth have arrived."

Was it Hope's imagination, or did she see a flicker of annoyance and trepidation on his face?

Whatever the expression was, it vanished immediately. Ewan got to his feet, smoothing out his waistcoat.

"I see. I'll be along directly."

Mr Golightly bowed and melted away from the doorway. Ewan swallowed hard, his eyes taking on a strange, inward-looking expression. Then his gaze fell on Hope, and he smiled mirthlessly.

"I suppose I'd better go and make small talk, then."

"Of course, your Grace." Hope replied. She hesitated; mouth open as if she wanted to say something else. The question – or statement, or whatever it was that her brain was cooking up – lingered on the tip of her tongue.

Hope closed her mouth and dropped a curtsey.

It's not Ewan, she reminded herself. It's the Duke.

Ewan dropped his gaze.

"Very well. Goodbye, Miss Barlow. And you, dearest, behave

yourself."

He bent down and pressed a kiss to Lucas' forehead, ruffling his hair. Then he was gone, striding away down the hallway. Hope listened to his footsteps receding, and wondered how she could ever have mistaken his quiet, light steps for the Dowager's.

***

A peal of laughter came from the half-open parlour door, and Ewan grimaced. He was conscious of feeling annoyed, disappointed that his conversation with Miss Barlow and time with Lucas had been cut short.

And then he was annoyed at that annoyance, knowing that he shouldn't be enjoying Miss Barlow's company that much. It was a slippery slope.

He tapped on the parlour door and stepped inside without waiting to be summoned. It was his house, after all.

Lady Harriet sat in the largest armchair they had, stirring her comically delicate teacup in her large hands. She was wearing a ruffled pink gown that wouldn't have suited anyone, and the gown glistened with diamonds and pearls. Ewan knew enough about the Emsworths to know that they would be real jewels, no paste nonsense.

Margaret occupied the second armchair, and Miss Viola Emsworth sat alone on the two-seater sofa.

She looked comically small next to her mother, and wore another ruffled dress, similar to her mother's, in a deep velvet. It suited her colouring and her slim frame, and from the way she sat and held herself, pouting as she stirred her own tea, she was very well aware of the fact.

All three of them looking up as Ewan stepped into the room. He noticed how Miss Viola's eyes lit up, her gaze flitting up and down his frame before dropping in affected modesty.

"Lady Emsworth, Miss Emsworth, welcome." Ewan said half-heartedly.

Lady Harriet chuckled. "Enough of the formality, please, your Grace! Do call me Lady Harriet. And Miss Viola or even Viola will do nicely for my daughter. We are all friends here, are we not?"

Ewan smiled tightly and said nothing.

"Sit down, Ewan, please." Margaret said brightly.

The only chair he could reasonably take was the second seat beside Miss Viola, which was no doubt the intention. Ewan briefly flirted with the idea of marching over to the window seat, and sitting there, but reluctantly decided against it.

Lady Harriet's smile widened when he sat beside Miss Viola.

"How lovely that we're all together again." She said brightly. "Viola, do tell his Grace about what happened to you in the milliner's the other day, and you met that impertinent shop-girl. I dare say you'll laugh yourself sick at this, your Grace."

His Grace doubted it very much.

Chapter Thirteen

Hope eyed her reflection in the mirror, chewing her lip.

There was a smear across the glass where a careless maid's cloth had made a smudge, distorting Hope's view of herself. She longed to get a cloth and clean it up herself, but there wasn't time now. She'd considered asking Mrs Golightly if she could have one of the maids clean it again, but that felt a little impertinent. After all, if the servants considered her one of them, they would be put out if they were asked to clean up after her. That would be a good way to make sure she had absolutely no friends in this house, upstairs or down.

Calm yourself, Hope, she told herself firmly. It's just a day out with your employer and your student. Nothing to worry about.

She'd chosen her lavender gown for the outing, since it was one of her best. It was pretty, but not eye-catchingly so. Not showy. Nobody wanted a showy governess, apparently.

It had been touching when Lucas asked if Hope could come along on their outing, but now Hope wished she could have stayed at home. How should she behave? What should she do?

Emily was coming along, so obviously Hope wasn't going to be solely responsible for Lucas.

Why had she been invited?

Ewan had behaved differently to her last time she saw him, though. Hope bit her lip, trying not to remember how he'd smiled up at her, how loving and affectionate he had been with Lucas. Whatever faults Ewan – the duke! – might have, he was certainly an excellent father.

Hope let out a breath, pulling a face at her own smeary reflection.

The lavender dress would have to do.

"He's almost ready." Emily said, chasing Lucas around the nursery with the final shoe. "He's been up since the crack of dawn, haven't you, Master Lucas?"

"We're going to see the animals!" Lucas trilled. "I can't wait! What's your favourite animal, Miss Barlow?"

"Goodness gracious, how could I choose?" Hope laughed. "I

think owls are my favourite animals. We learned about owls the other day, didn't we?"

"They can turn their heads all the way around!"

"That's right. Now, why don't you let Emily put on your shoe, then we can go downstairs and meet your Papa."

Lucas collapsed in a heap, beaming and out of breath. Emily plumped down in front of him and began to pull on his shoe.

"It's not just the Duke coming with us today," Emily said, her voice low. "Just a word of warning."

A prickle of dread rolled down Hope's spine. She'd imagined a nice, quiet family day out, where she didn't have to worry too much about doing or saying the wrong thing.

"Is the Dowager coming?" Hope asked carelessly, heart pounding.

"Yes, and her two guests besides."

She frowned. "Guests?"

"Yes, some hoity-toity lady and her spoiled brat of a daughter. I don't recall their names, but they've got their noses stuck in the air." Emily scoffed. "I only caught a glimpse of them, but I think they're here to stay for a while, judging by all the trunks and bags they brought along with them."

Hope's heart sank. This was all she needed – two Society ladies along with the Dowager, here to hang over her shoulder and watch her every move.

"What does hoity-toity mean?" Lucas inquired.

"Never you mind." Emily said with a grin, leaning forward to pinch his nose. "Don't you repeat what we say, young Master Lucas. You are too sharp for your own good."

"So sharp I'll cut myself?" Lucas asked, giggling and squirming.

"Even so."

Emily got to her feet, shaking out her skirts. She let out a sigh and glanced over at Hope.

"I suppose we'd better go down, then. They won't be happy if they're kept waiting for the likes of us."

"No," Hope murmured. "I don't suppose they will."

The foyer was a hive of activity, with footmen dashing to and fro. The main door was open, revealing a cool, grey day outside, the sun bright despite the clouds. Two carriages waited on the drive. One would be for Lucas, his governess, and his nursemaid, and the other would be for the Dowager and her two guests, Hope realized. She wondered which carriage Ewan would take.

The one with his mother and guests, of course.

"Can't we go now, Miss Barlow?" Lucas asked, holding onto both Hope and Emily's hands, peering up at them. "I'm all ready."

"We have to wait for your papa and grandmama." Hope said, smiling down at him. "Just a few more minutes, I'm sure."

Lucas pouted, hopping from foot to foot. Hope pulled her shawl a little more tightly around herself and hoped that Ewan would arrive soon. The little boy was getting fidgety.

Where are they all? I wish they'd hurry, Hope thought, immediately followed by, be careful what you wish for, you fool.

Upstairs, there was a cacophony of doors slamming and brisk, ladylike footsteps. The Dowager led the way down the stairs, resplendent in a black silk gown and pearls.

She was followed by two women that Hope did, unfortunately, recognize.

Lady Harriet Emsworth had draped her bulk in an alarmingly yellow chiffon gown, and her sharp, clever eyes raked everywhere, missing nothing. Her daughter, Miss Viola, swept down the stairs after her mother, regal and elegant in a gown studded with sequins, beads, and other decorations. Underneath all of that, Hope guessed that it was a pale blue.

"I see you have young Master Lucas ready." The Dowager breezed, crossing the foyer to stop in front of Hope and Lucas. "Lucas, darling, are you well? Are you warm enough?"

"Yes, Grandmama." Lucas chirped up. "Are we going now?"

"In a moment, dearest. Your papa will be down shortly." The Dowager's gaze flicked up from Lucas to Hope, and her pleasant expression melted away. "You should not have brought him to stand so close to the open door. Do you not feel that draft, Miss Barlow?"

"Miss Barlow? Wait, you don't mean..." Miss Viola chirped up in a stage whisper, only to receive an elbow in the ribs from her mother, and hastily bit off the rest of her sentence.

Hope held her breath, but fortunately the Dowager did not seem to have heard. She glanced over Lucas' clothing, obviously deeming it satisfactory, and turned on her heel, moving back over to her guests.

She didn't bother to introduce them to Hope and Emily, of course. Why would she?

It didn't matter, either way. Hope had recognized them both at once, and it was obvious that they recognized her.

The Emsworth family had never been friends of the Barlow family, and Hope and Viola had always disliked each other. Hope considered Viola to be vain, spoilt, and downright malicious at times. Their paths had crossed often, unfortunately, mostly at balls, soirees, parties, and during promenades in the Park.

That was before Hope's family fell from grace, of course. Since then, she hadn't seen hide nor hair of any of the Emsworth family. She'd assumed that Miss Viola was married, but now it seemed otherwise.

She must be getting desperate, Hope thought. She kept her gaze levelled discreetly down at the tiles beneath her feet and prayed that Ewan would arrive before Lucas got too fidgety and decided to run around. Somehow, Hope knew that any misbehavior on the part of her charge would be levelled directly at her.

With a start, she realized that the Dowager was talking about her. Putting her own daydreams and worries to one side, Hope concentrated on listening in.

"… entirely too young." The Dowager was saying. "Lucas is fond of her already – he is such a sweet boy – but only time will tell if she's up to our standards, of course."

"Of course," Lady Harriet echoed. "A young governess is not to be trusted, I'm afraid. When my Viola was young, we must have gone through dozens of governesses. Did we not, darling?"

"Oh, dozens," Viola chirped. "They were all wretchedly stupid. Lord, how I used to plague them. Do you remember, Mama?"

"I remember. None of them were fit to control her. I don't believe a wrote a single good reference during the whole of Viola's schooling. In the end we just sent her off to a finishing school in Paris. Such a higher standard of education, don't you agree?"

"I would agree, but we aren't ready to send Lucas off to boarding school yet." The Dowager said, sounding hesitant. "So, I'm afraid there's nothing that can be done about the governess."

Lady Harriet took a step closer to the Dowager, dropping her voice under the pretense of secrecy, but in reality, not low enough to be out of Hope's earshot.

"I should get rid of the young wench if I were you. I can recommend some very good governesses and tutors."

The Dowager sighed. "I must give her a chance, Harriet."

"Tosh. You can't worry too much about the feelings of these people."

Hope lifted her eyes from the ground and found that Lady Harriet was staring directly at her. It was apparent that she'd been recognized. Lady Harriet immediately averted her gaze, making no attempt at all to show any acknowledgement of Hope's presence. The Dowager glanced up too, seeming to realize that Hope had heard their conversation. She, at least, had the grace to blush.

Viola had already gotten bored and had wandered across the foyer to gawp at some paintings on the wall.

"Do we have to wait much longer?" she snapped, turning around to glare at her mother.

Then heavy footsteps sounded from further up along the hall, and Viola seemed to come to life. She perked up, dashing back to the main group, and swept a complacent palm over her hair. Her hair was, of course, immaculately and fashionably dressed, with tiny jewels glittering in the depths of her curls. Hope resisted the urge to lift her hand to her own hair, which was pulled back in a simple knot, without any adornments at all, and had been put up with her own hands, peering into a single, smeary mirror.

Ewan appeared, walking briskly, dressed in a plain brown walking-suit and Hessians.

"Sorry to keep you waiting." He said lightly, flashing a smile all round. His gaze caught on Hope's, and for an instant she was sure that all the air had been sucked out of the room.

Then his gaze passed on, and everything returned to normal. Hope dropped her eyes, feeling rather foolish.

"Oh, not at all, your Grace." Viola simpered. "We've only just arrived, haven't we, Mama?"

"I'm sure your Grace is worth the wait." Lady Harriet agreed, smiling coyly.

"Patience is a virtue, after all." Viola added, glancing at her mother for approval. She sidled a little closer to Ewan, as if she wanted to casually lay her hand on his arm.

Ewan moved away to greet Lucas, sweeping him up into his arms for a hug.

"Good morning, my sweet boy," Ewan murmured, pressing a kiss to Lucas' forehead. "Are you ready to see the Tower? And the animals?"

"I can't wait, Papa!" Lucas agreed, beaming. "Are we leaving now?"

"Yes, we shall leave at once."

"I'm not sure there's much need for Emily and Miss Barlow to come." The Dowager said lightly, her gaze dwelling on Hope.

Ewan shrugged. "We're already going to need two carriages, so they might as well come and see the animals and the Tower, too."

Lady Harriet and Viola exchanged glances, and Viola let out a calculated peal of laughter.

"Oh, your Grace, you are too much! Is it a day out for the servants, too? Am I to share a carriage with the cook and all the scullery maids? Are they going to bring the kitchen scraps to feed the animals? How very droll."

Ewan didn't like that. He was facing Hope, keeping his back to his mother and his guests, and she saw a tightness come across his expression. Their eyes met for a split second, and Hope could have sworn she saw an apology there.

"Lucas is keen for his nursemaid and his governess to come." Ewan said shortly, carefully setting Lucas back down on his feet.

"Goodness." Lady Harriet remarked. "So young, and already he rules the roost."

She'd spoken in an undertone, but just like before, her voice was still loud enough for everyone to hear. Hope wasn't entirely sure whether she meant to be overheard, or just had no idea how loud she really was.

Ewan's expression turned thunderous for a moment. He met Hope's eyes again, and she widened them, hoping to convey the importance of staying calm.

The thunder faded away. For now, at least. Ewan pasted on a smile and turned to face his guests.

"Right, shall we decide what we're doing next, then?"

Chapter Fourteen

Ewan had seen it. Just for a split second, he saw the challenge in Lady Harriet's eyes. She was daring him to say something, to shame himself and be impolite to a guest in his own house.

He'd caught the look on Hope's face. She was almost pleading with him to stay calm and not rise to the bait, and she was right.

He smiled, tight-lipped, not reaching his eyes, and some of Lady Harriet's smugness faded away.

"I understand you are not coming with us, Mother?"

"No, gawping at animals and inspecting various dungeons is not my idea of a good time." The Dowager remarked acidly. "Lady Harriet, Miss Emsworth, and I will be going shopping instead."

"How enjoyable." Ewan said, not sounding sincere in the slightest. "I wish you joy."

"I was thinking, your Grace," Miss Viola said, stepping forward at a significant look from her mother, "Why don't you accompany us? Since the nursemaid and the governess both insist upon coming, why not let them take care of sweet Lucas while we adults enjoy some of the more... refined enjoyments of the town? What say you?"

Ewan blinked. "I am sorry to disappoint you, Miss Viola, but I'm afraid I have promised Lucas that I would accompany him. This is our time, you see."

Miss Viola flinched, seeming taken aback. This was obviously a young lady who wasn't used to hearing no. If a person was clever enough and phrased their request in polite enough language – and a public enough space – it was very difficult for their request to be denied.

But this was not a public space. It was Ewan's home, and he'd be damned if he let a whiny brat like Viola Emsworth keep him from his son.

"Oh, come, Ewan, I'm sure you could spend a little time with us." Margaret wheedled. "After all, when you promised Lucas to take him to the Tower, you didn't know about our guests. I'm sure you won't mind, will you, Lucas? Don't be impolite, Ewan." She added, sotto voce.

Margaret glanced down at Lucas, an encouraging smile on her face. Lucas' gaze darted between the adults, a look of disappointment on his little face. He lifted his chin and put a weak smile on his face.

"I don't mind if you want to go shopping instead, Papa. If that's what you want, I really don't mind." He said lamely.

Ewan crouched down before Lucas.

"Do you remember how I said I would always keep my word to you, no matter what?" Ewan said, his voice low.

Lucas nodded.

"Well, I meant it. I would not rather go shopping than go to the Tower with you, Lucas, but even if I did, I would still rather spend time with you, do you understand?" he reached out, ruffling Lucas' hair. "Our plans still stand, my boy."

Lucas beamed.

Conscious of eyes on him, Ewan glanced up, catching Hope's gaze. She was looking at him with a strange, speculative expression on her face, and hastily looked away when their eyes met.

Swallowing hard, Ewan rose to his feet and turned back to his mother and the guests.

"As I'm sure you heard, my engagement with Lucas still stands." Ewan said acidly. "I'm sorry for any disappointment."

Margaret had gone red, obviously embarrassed. She kept glancing at Lady Harriet, a little shame-facedly. Lady Harriet's face gave away nothing.

Miss Viola, on the other hand, clearly did not know when to stop.

"Oh, do come with us, your Grace!" she wheedled. "I should dearly enjoy your company. I promise I shall make it worth your while. After all, it's not as if you'll enjoy such agreeable company and conversation with those filthy, smelly animals."

She gave a titter of laughter at this, glancing back at her mother for encouragement.

Ewan bit back on a sharp retort, something about the animals being much better company. Instead, he gave a brittle smile, and disengaged his arm from Miss Viola's.

"We had better get in the carriages, I think." He said brightly. "As I said before, Miss Viola, I really cannot come. Another time, perhaps."

He turned away on pretense of speaking to Golightly about something. He caught a flash of sympathy on the butler's face before it was discreetly wiped away.

There was a general clatter of footsteps and murmurs of chatter as the group headed towards the door. The lead carriage, the nicest one, was to take Margaret and her guests into town, and the second-best carriage would go to the Tower.

As if conjured by magic, Margaret appeared at his elbow.

"You didn't need to be so sharp with Viola." She said shortly. "I was quite mortified, Ewan."

"Mother, I should be ashamed to harangue a person like Miss Viola has just done. I am spending a day out with my son, for heaven's sake!"

Golightly discreetly melted away, leaving Ewan and Margaret to talk.

Margaret was clearly angry. The pink flush hadn't quite left her face. She folded her arms tightly across her chest.

"I love Lucas quite as much as you, and I don't believe that you would do him any harm by sending him off with the nursemaid and Miss Barlow. You are too nice about these things, Ewan. He'll be perfectly safe."

"That's not at all the problem. I want to spend time with my son."

Margaret sighed. "Your father never bothered about that, did he? He didn't take you on silly outings and trips, neglecting his guests because of childish promises. It did you no harm."

"I want to be a different sort of father to my son, Mother. I'm not pleased that you keep going on about this. I'm sorry to disappoint Lady Harriet and Miss Viola, but it's not as if they came here to see me."

A flash of guilt crossed Margaret's face, and she hastily averted her gaze. Ewan frowned, narrowing his eyes.

"Mother?"

"Hm?"

"Why are they here?"

"I told you." Margaret replied distractedly. "The hotel, and..."

"Mother, let me tell you now, that if Miss Viola has hopes of me, she'll be disappointed."

The colour rushed back into Margaret's face. "Well, Ewan, that is quite a leap to make! Of course, Miss Viola is a suitable, eligible lady. She is very accomplished, extremely pretty, and so very charming."

"She's insufferable."

"Ewan!" Margaret glanced over her shoulder, making sure that their guests weren't within earshot.

They weren't fortunately. Ewan could see that Lady Harriet and Miss Viola had made their way out into the courtyard, and Lady Harriet was currently heaving herself into the carriage. Hope stood back, unobtrusive, holding Lucas' hand. Lucas was chattering to her about something or other, excited and animated, and Hope was listening carefully, interjecting occasionally.

Something warmed Ewan's heart, something that he hadn't felt for quite a while.

He cleared his throat, looking away. Hope – Miss Barlow, he reminded himself – was just doing her job. She was a governess, and a rather good one, too. Lucas liked her, and that was good. It didn't mean anything. If life had been different, it might have been Caroline out there, holding her son's hand.

But it's not, Ewan thought dizzily. Caroline is gone, and wishing it was otherwise won't make the slightest bit of difference.

"Ewan? Are you listening to me?"

"Yes, Mother." Ewan lied. "I'm sorry to disappoint them, I truly am, but this is not up for discussion."

Margaret sighed, shaking her head. She nibbled on her lower lip, considering.

"Well, at least ride in the carriage with us. That way, you can have some conversation with Miss Viola. She is very fond of you, you know."

"I think she's fond of my title, and my money, and this house."

"Don't be so vulgar. Come, let's go."

Ewan shook his head. "There's no point in me riding in your carriage."

"That's hardly relevant. We can have the coach driver drop you off near the Tower, and Miss Barlow and Emily can ride with Lucas."

"I would like to ride with Lucas, Mother."

"Ewan, don't be difficult."

A flash of anger shot through him, and Ewan drew in a few deep breaths, calming himself.

"Don't speak to me like I'm a child." He said, his voice low and level. "I am the Duke of Darenwood, Mother. I am a grown man, and I make my own decisions."

Margaret swallowed hard, lifting her chin. "And I'm not to give you any advice at all, am I?"

"Of course you may. I welcome your advice, Mother. But I don't promise to take it regardless of what I think myself. Otherwise, I'm not taking advice, I'm simply taking orders. Now, if you'll excuse me, I've kept my son waiting long enough."

Ewan stepped back his mother, walking across the foyer and out into the cool, bright light of the day.

He felt guilty, of course, for speaking so sharply to his mother, but otherwise she really just wouldn't listen.

Don't make excuses, he told himself. Make it up to her later.

And he would, of course. Later.

Miss Viola perked up as she saw him approach. Lady Harriet had just settled herself in the carriage.

"Oh, are you coming with us after all, your Grace?"

Ewan smiled tightly. "No, Miss Viola. I hope you have an enjoyable outing, and I shall see you all this afternoon."

He gave a brief bow, not so shallow as to be impolite, but not a particularly deep and respectful one, either. Miss Viola pouted but turned to climb into the carriage.

Ewan turned to the second carriage. Emily climbed in first, helping Lucas to climb after her. Hope hung back, watching him with a smile.

"He's terribly excited." She said, glancing briefly up at Ewan. "I'm glad you're still coming with us. I think you coming was just as exciting for Master Lucas as the Tower and the animals."

Ewan suppressed a smile. "What sort of father would I be if I chose shopping over my own son?"

"A bad one, I suppose." Hope said, with a short laugh. She was smiling a little more freely now, and it occurred to Ewan that there'd been a sort of tenseness about her while she stood in the foyer with Lady Harriet and Miss Viola.

Well, that was to be expected, really.

Lucas settled himself in his seat, beaming out at them.

"Come on, slow-pokes!" he chirped.

Ewan chuckled. "After you, Miss Barlow."

She flashed a quick smile at him and moved towards the carriage.

This was a high-sprung one, with two steps up into it. It was a fine carriage, but one designed for quickly making one's way around the town and country, not for family trips out. Hope pinched her skirts, lifting her hems enough to climb into the carriage.

Then Ewan noticed the footman.

The footmen came out to escort the guests and family into the carriages of course, unobtrusive in their green and gold livery. Ewan didn't recognize this young man – Golightly was always hiring new footmen – but he was younger than the rest. He was probably handsome, too, under the wig and starchy uniform.

He was watching Hope intently, his gaze lingering on her longer than was proper.

"Let me help you, miss." The footman said – he should not have been speaking, and normally that would not bother Ewan, but now it did – and stepped forward, holding out a white-gloved hand.

He still had that intent look on his face, and Ewan realized with a foolish rush that the footman thought she was pretty. Well, of course he would. Who would not think Hope Barlow was pretty?

Hope flashed him a shy smile, moving to take his hand and climb into the carriage.

"I shall help her." Ewan heard himself say, standing forward.

The footman flushed, dropping his gaze and moving back.

Hope glanced back over her shoulder at him, one eyebrow raised. Ewan extended his own hand – ungloved – and waited.

She hesitated, and Ewan wondered whether she was deciding whether to reject his offer of help, or whether she should take her chances climbing into the carriage herself.

The decision was made. Hope took his hand and climbed up.

Her skin was warm and soft against it. Not quite as soft and white as ladies' hands were supposed to be. Hers were the flexible, strong hands of a woman used to sewing, writing, doing things, not the dainty, lily-white fingers of a lady who lifted nothing heavier than a teacup to her lips.

The touch sent sparks flying down Ewan's arm, almost taking his breath away.

Then the instant was gone. Hope let go of his hand, settling herself into the carriage, and there was nothing for Ewan to do but clamber up after her. His hand still tingled from where Hope had touched it, and he clenched his hand into a fist to get rid of the sensation.

Once they were inside and the door was locked, Ewan leaned back, closing his eyes. The carriage lurched forward, and they were on their way. Lucas gave a squeal of delight, leaning out of the window to wave goodbye to the house.

Ewan tried not to look at Hope, who was seated opposite him.

Think of Caroline, he told himself firmly.

Chapter Fifteen

Lucas was in fine, high spirits.

"Can we see the animals first?" he asked hopefully, as the carriage rattled to a halt.

"Of course we can." Ewan replied, laughing.

Hope forced a smile, but her thoughts were elsewhere. Was it her imagination, or had Ewan's behavior been a little... a little strange?

Why insist on helping her into the carriage himself? That wasn't the sort of thing dukes did for governesses. The footman had been going to help her up, why did Ewan intervene?

Perhaps it was just a whim, or a passing fancy, Hope thought. After all, he's a duke now. He can indulge whatever whims he likes.

Somehow, that thought was... disappointing? Hope bit her lip, deciding not to try and make sense of it all. They'd arrived, anyway.

They could hear the animals and their cacophony from a distance. Hope held onto one of Lucas' hands, and Ewan held the other. Emily followed behind, craning her neck to gawp at the sights.

Crowds of sightseers clustered around them, all chatting and laughing, all moving forward in the same direction. Usually, Hope would feel ill at ease in crowds. Somehow, though, it didn't feel quite as worrying with Ewan there. He was tall and confident, walking through the crowds as if he expected them to part for him and let him through. And they did.

"We ought to enjoy today," Ewan said, leading them down a narrower, quieter pathway. "We may not always be able to come here and look at the animals."

Lucas glanced up inquisitively. "Why not?"

Ewan smiled softly. "I'll show you."

Lifting Lucas up so he could peer over a wall, Ewan pointed out the elephant enclosure. It was a large space, but somehow not quite large enough for the vast beast. The creature paced up and down listlessly, its comically delicate ears hanging down on either side of its head.

"Do you see the elephant?" Ewan asked.

"I see it, Papa!"

"It's big, isn't it."

"Very big."

"Do you think that enclosure is large enough for it?"

Lucas considered, nibbling his lower lip. "No." he said eventually. "I don't think so. But you'd need a big, big enclosure for it to be big enough, wouldn't you?"

Ewan nodded. "Exactly. Elephants are meant to roam free over vast plains in India and Africa. They're meant to be free. It's the same with all of the animals – the lions, tiger, cheetahs, baboons, all the animals here. Some are happy enough, but most – like that elephant – aren't happy here. They're sad, and that's a terrible shame, isn't it."

Lucas nodded. "We should let the animals go, shouldn't we?"

"We should, but certainly not in the middle of London, eh?" Ewan chuckled, setting Lucas down on his feet. "Now then, my little man, where to next?"

"I want to see the tigers!"

"Of you go, then!"

Lucas went haring off down the path, with Emily scurrying after him. That left Ewan and Hope walking together, side by side. She glanced up at him, not daring to let her gaze linger too long on his face.

"Is it true, then?" she said, not entirely sure when she'd decided to speak. "About the Menagerie closing down?"

Ewan glanced briefly down at her, not long enough for their eyes to meet.

"There's talk of it. Time will tell whether that's all it is – just talk. What do you think about it all? There'll be an outcry, I'm sure."

Hope considered. "It would be sad, in a way. Losing the Menagerie, which is a place of wonder and marvels for many of us. On the other hand, it's the best thing to do for the animals. Besides, I often wonder how well the animals are cared for here."

"Oh, well enough, I should think. There's just the matter of space, I imagine. And, after all, a tiger who's used to hunting through miles of jungle to bring down their own prey is likely to be bored with hunks of meat thrown his way every day."

"That is a good point." Hope admitted, a smile twitching at the corners of his mouth.

They walked on, Lucas and Emily circling ahead of them, peering at things over the wall and exclaiming to each other.

"I'm sorry about all that business today." Ewan said abruptly. "I believe Lady Harriet likes to make people uncomfortable."

Hope bit down on a response. I know, she wanted to say. I've known her for a while, and she's always been an awful woman.

"It's quite alright." Hope said instead.

"No, it wasn't. I saw how uncomfortable you and Emily were. Besides, I wasn't pleased with my mother trying to make Lucas give up his day out with me. And for what? For shopping with two ladies that I don't even like." There was a brief pause, and Ewan grimaced. "I shouldn't have said that."

Hope glanced down at her feet.

"It's alright. I could see how distressed it made you. I suppose the Dowager only wants to take care of her guests."

"I suppose so. Still, I won't be put on the spot like that in my own house. Perhaps if I'd have some other engagement, I've have changed my plans to oblige my guests, but not this. Not my son."

Hope looked up at him again, as if her gaze was drawn by magnetism. Ewan was looking straight ahead, his face set and almost angry. A lock of hair had fallen forward over his forehead, and Hope was struck with the sudden, powerful desire to reach up and brush it back.

She did no such thing, of course. Hope curled her hands into fists and placed them behind her back so as to get the thought out of her mind.

What are you doing, fool? She scolded herself. This isn't the Ewan you were friends with as a child. Things are different now. Why can't you understand that? Make no mistake, you'll be dismissed in a heartbeat if you act badly or make a false step. Don't get comfortable.

Up ahead, something happened to jerk Hope out of her maudlin reverie.

Lucas caught his foot on an uneven cobblestone, and toppled over before Emily could catch him. He climbed to his feet, mouth twisted down, chin wobbling. Emily held out her hands to him, but Lucas turned and raced back towards Hope and Ewan.

He went straight to Hope.

"I scraped my hand, Miss Barlow!" Lucas said, tears of shock and anger glimmering in his eyes. "It hurts."

Hope crouched down before him, taking out a clean handkerchief.

"Let me take a look. Oh, it's not so bad! See, it's just a tiny graze."

"It hurts."

"You'll have a nasty bruise, but that's all. See, there's not even any blood. I shall wipe away some of the grit, and you must be careful in future, but that's all. No harm done."

Some of the pain dissolved from Lucas' face. He sniffled, watching Hope wipe away the grit and dirt from his palm. He flexed his hand, inspecting the graze for blood and other debris. Finding none, he turned on his heel, satisfied, and set off as fast as before.

"I beg your pardon, your Grace." Emily said, hovering nearby. "I'll keep a closer eye on him in future."

"It wasn't your fault, Emily." Ewan replied. "Please don't worry about it. Besides, as Miss Barlow said, there's no harm done."

Relieved, Emily dashed away after her charge, leaving Hope and Ewan alone again.

Or as alone as two people could be, in the middle of the Royal Menagerie.

She could feel Ewan's eyes on her. Hope got to her feet, shaking out her handkerchief and putting it away.

"You have a remarkable knack with children, Miss Barlow." Ewan said. "I envy you."

"You envy me?" Hope couldn't help repeating, her voice incredulous.

"Yes, I do. When Lucas was born, I had no idea what to do. I didn't even know how to hold a baby, let alone manage a screaming one. When he started to toddle around, speak, and ask questions, I was entirely at a loss. And, because I am a man, nobody seemed to think that I needed these skills. As if they thought I should be entirely disinterested in my own children. It made me angry, to tell the truth. Some men of my acquaintance told me that they saw their children once or twice a week, if that, and rarely had a conversation with them. They saw nothing at all wrong with it, but... well, that's not the sort of father I want to be."

Hope swallowed hard. A lump was forming in her throat, and she knew exactly what had put it there.

It was longing.

For a few brief seconds, as she consoled Lucas and inspected his tiny injury, it almost felt like he was her child.

Was this how governesses felt? That the children they were charged with caring for were their own? If so, how did it feel when the children grew up and lost interest in their governesses, or when the family they lived with decided in the space of a day or two that a governess was no longer needed and she was to pack her things and go before the next morning, thank you very much?

Hope cleared her throat, conscious that Ewan's eyes were on her.

"Well, I envy you, your Grace. And not for the obvious reasons, either. You have Lucas. He's the sweetest child I've ever met, and I frankly love him. So does everyone else, by the way."

Ewan smiled proudly. "I know. He's a dear boy. I am proud of him. Did you expect to have children of your own, then?"

Hope kept a light smile on her face, although it was getting harder by the minute.

"Yes, I did. Of course, that hasn't happened. It's just one of those things, you know? There are plenty of other things to do in life. Besides, I'm far too busy."

Ewan said nothing in response to this, and Hope was secretly grateful.

She couldn't pinpoint where the longing had started. As a child, when she'd been friends with Ewan, Hope had preferred tin soldiers and teddy bears to baby dolls. Somewhere along the line, though, a desire for her own child, her own family had come into being. These days, it was more powerful than ever, made stronger by the fact that she could not have it.

Who would marry me? Hope thought listlessly. *I have no dowry, no prospects, no friends. If I don't marry a man of Quality, I'll be lost to the world I know forever. I suppose that wouldn't be the worst thing, but I'd never see Ewan again.*

To her surprise, that idea sent a pang of misery shooting through her chest.

Never see Ewan again? Unthinkable.

"I think we should catch up with them." Ewan said lightly. "There's lots to see, and we'd better get organized."

***

The next few hours went by in a flurry of beasts and birds, each new spectacle more thrilling than the last. Lions, tigers, baboons, zebras, and more all regarded the crowds as curiously as they themselves were being looked at.

"There was a polar bear here, once." Ewan said, lifting Lucas up to see a huge brown bear far below. "It was allowed to swim in the lakes and rivers and eat fish. On a chain, of course."

Hope frowned, imagining a huge white bear on a leash. It didn't seem right, somehow.

"I like looking at the animals." Lucas said seriously, "But you're right, Papa. They don't have a lot of room. I'd be sad if I couldn't come and see the animals anymore, but I'd be happy if they were free."

"That's my good, kind boy." Ewan said, kissing his temple. "Now, onto the Tower. Miss Barlow, do you remember when we were children, and you believed that there was a princess locked up in the Tower of London?"

Hope flinched, blinking in surprise at the memory.

"Yes, I do." She answered without thinking. "I used to draw pictures of her. She wore a long, bright-green dress, and had the longest, reddest hair in the world. I am surprised you remembered, your Grace."

Hope was suddenly conscious of Emily, standing behind her, gaze flicking between Hope and Ewan. Emily said nothing, of course, but Hope knew that she was listening.

Ewan chuckled. "That's not the sort of thing a person forgets, Miss Barlow. Do you think your princess has escaped by now? Maybe tossed her long hair out of the window and used it as a pulley to lower herself to the ground?"

Hope had to smile at that. "I'm sure she has escaped. If not, she must be terribly sad and lonely."

Ewan's gaze met herself for a breathless instant. "Well, we wouldn't want that."

Then he turned away, leading the way down a bridge which led to the dark Tower, looming over them.

"I don't like that." Lucas stated. He had his arms around his father's shoulders, and the two painted the most delightful domestic picture that Hope could have imagined. "It's not fair to keep a princess locked up like that. Somebody should try and get her out."

Chapter Sixteen

The shopping trip was not a success. Margaret wasn't sure what she had expected, really.

Viola was in a bad mood because Ewan hadn't come with them, and Lady Harriet seemed displeased that he wasn't as easy to command as she'd hoped.

I tried to tell her, Margaret thought, folding her arms tightly. Ewan isn't some timid, vapid youth, tied to his mother's apron strings. He's a grown man and a father.

They were heading home now, with Viola complaining incessantly over how much the carriage was rattling her around. Nobody was paying any attention to her, which made her complain louder.

Margaret privately thought that their journey home would have been more comfortable if the wretched girl hadn't filled the carriage with bandboxes and bags. Why did she need to buy so much? She'd brought at least four trunks with her!

No, stop, Margaret told herself, drawing in a deep breath. Viola is disappointed, that's all. She's a good girl at heart, you know that. Besides, this is exactly what you and Harriet wanted. Our families, united. It's a perfect match, and it'll be good for us all. Once Ewan gets over his pique, everything will be fine.

If he gets over his pique, of course.

The bright, grey day was turning dark, and they would have rain soon. Margaret sighed with relief when they sighted the long, winding gravel drive that led home. It felt as if they had wasted the day shopping.

"I shall rest when I get home, Mama." Viola announced, tossing her curls. "I'm quite tired out."

"Of course, dearest." Lady Harriet said, leaning forward to pat her daughter's knee. "Just don't be late for dinner."

"Will his Grace be joining us?" Viola asked, in an off-handed tone that fooled nobody.

Margaret answered, forcing a smile.

"Of course, my dear."

"How lovely. We've hardly seen him since we arrived." Lady Harriet stated, leaning back in her seat again. "If I didn't know better, I'd say that he was avoiding us."

Margaret didn't meet her friend's eye, instead focusing on a loose thread at her sleeve. She would have a word with Ewan and insist that he spend more time with their guests. Really, it was ridiculous.

"You know how busy my son can be." Margaret said lightly. "I'm sure he's as disappointed as you are."

There was a long silence, and Margaret was just starting to fidget when Lady Harriet spoke.

"I wonder if you and I could take tea together in the parlour, once we arrive home?" Lady Harriet said. "Viola will be resting, and no doubt his Grace will be otherwise occupied. We shall enjoy a lovely conversation, you and I."

"I should like that very much." Margaret lied.

The rain was just starting up as they exited the carriage. Viola gave a shriek, darting inside at the first hints of rain, saying something about her hair, her gown, and her shoes.

Margaret paused, glancing over at the second carriage, which was just parked in front of them. Ewan and Lucas must have just arrived home.

Lucas was standing on the steps in front of the house, holding out a slightly grazed palm. Miss Barlow was inspecting it, saying something that made Lucas laugh.

Emily was in the process of getting the rest of the things out of the carriage, and Ewan stood over Miss Barlow and Lucas. There was a strange look on his face. Margaret paused, frowning, and looked a little closer. None of them had noticed her, not yet at least.

Ewan's expression was soft, his eyes distant, and there was a gentle smile on his face. He was glancing between Lucas and Miss Barlow, as if he didn't know who to dwell on the most.

As she watched, Lucas lurched forward, wrapping Miss Barlow in a tight hug. The girl laughed and hugged him back. The expression in Ewan's eyes had turned to something horrifyingly tender.

Margaret sucked in a breath, hastily turning her back. She couldn't possibly let Harriet see. Lady Harriet was her friend, but Margaret was under no illusions as to what would happen if she sniffed out some juicy gossip. The Duke of Darenwood taking a fancy to a governess would be shocking fare for the scandal sheets. They'd be talking about it all Season, and the next.

The gossip would be even more malicious, the scandal even worse if the Duke had recently spurned Lady Harriet's perfectly suitable daughter.

Thankfully, Lady Harriet was not looking. She was busying herself with climbing out of the carriage, and when Margaret glanced back again, Lucas and Miss Barlow were going inside, followed by Ewan. She let out a breath she hadn't even realized that she was holding.

Lady Harriet got her feet on the floor with a sigh of relief.

"Margaret, I shall change and then meet you in the parlour. What say you?"

"Of course, Harriet." Margaret replied mildly. "Whatever you like."

***

They sat in silence and drank their tea for what seemed like an interminably long time.

"I am terribly sorry that Ewan wouldn't accompany us today." Margaret said, breaking the silence first. "He so dotes on Lucas."

Lady Harriet's expression remained impassive. "He's not a man to be easily controlled. I can understand that. It just means that we must put forward a little extra effort."

More silence. More tea sipping. Margaret helped herself to a piece of cake, and then immediately wished she hadn't. Her mouth was too dry, and the cake seemed to stick, going down her gullet like a lump of sawdust. She chewed and swallowed diligently, trying not to let Lady Harriet's unflinching gaze worry her.

"Why did you invite us here, Margaret?" Lady Harriet said, once Margaret had managed her last swallow.

"I beg your pardon?"

Lady Harriet set down her teacup with a clack. "Let's not beat about the bush. We are women of the world, you and I. We understand how the tiresome business of the marriage mart goes along, and we understand that sometimes, the older folks – the mammas and papas of the world – must intervene to make sure things go smoothly."

"Yes, I couldn't agree more."

"I inferred from your letter that a match could be set up between my Viola and his Grace. I hate to be so blunt, Margaret, but I don't like the idea that we may be at cross purposes here."

Margaret flushed, putting down her teacup too.

"You are right, Harriet. That was my intention. I must say, I prefer having things out in the open like this. It makes things simpler, in my opinion."

Lady Harriet pursed her lips. "I assumed that his Grace was also pleased with this arrangement. Now, I feel that he is… distracted. The pretty governess is not a welcome addition."

"We'd intended to hire a much older woman. Someone more suitable…"

"And yet, you didn't. You hired Miss Barlow. That girl is unsuitable for this role in more ways than one, which I shan't go into here." Lady Harriet sighed, shaking her head. "When his Grace made that scene this morning in the foyer, I considered packing our things and leaving at once."

A flash of panic went through Margaret. Having Lady Harriet as a friend was a dangerous thing, but having her as an enemy was much, much worse.

"Oh, Harriet, please don't talk like that. I'm sure Ewan never meant any offence."

"I think I shall be the judge of that, if you don't mind."

Silence fell once again. Margaret forced herself to wait for Lady Harriet to speak.

They were taking tea in the Good Parlour, which was how Margaret referred to the small, uncomfortable, and impeccably decorated parlour on the south side of the house, commanding plenty of light and an unparalleled view of the landscape, seen through a huge picture window. It was a place to discuss serious matters, business, and extremely secret secrets, so it seemed appropriate for this discussion.

Now, though, Margaret was regretting her choice. Her chair was overstuffed and uncomfortable, and the coffee table was set just a little too far away and a fraction of an inch too low down to be truly comfortable. It was as if the room had been designed for inconvenience.

"I don't believe that his Grace intends to marry." Lady Harriet said slowly. "I'd assumed that he was looking, at least, but now... well, I don't know what to think."

Margaret had been expecting this. "Ewan has been mourning Caroline for many years. He's now starting to be more like himself. He talked about Lucas, and how the poor boy is missing a mother-figure in his life. Besides that, I know very well that Ewan is lonely. Why should he not marry again? I worry that when Ewan finally does cast his eyes about to marry, he'll be snatched up by the first wide-eyed chit who gets her hooks into him. It could be anyone. Some fortuneless, conniving girl with a little beauty and less brains, or... or worse." Margaret couldn't bring herself to finish that sentence. "Caroline was a real catch. I can't bear for Ewan to match below what he deserves. In my opinion, it would be better to get ahead of all this and secure his marriage to a suitable girl before he can start to notice all the unsuitable ones. He's just proving more... more stubborn than I'd expected."

Lady Harriet considered this, nodding slowly. She leaned forward, pouring out two fresh cups of tea.

"Thank you for being so honest, my dear friend. You're right, you know. Men can be so obtuse at times, and young men are the worst. With daughters, a parent can put their foot down, and simply insist that they do something – or don't do something. It results in a lot of tears and silliness, but at least the girls can be compelled. With sons... well. That's a little different. Some subterfuge is required."

Margaret winced. "I don't shine when it comes to that, I'm afraid."

Lady Harriet smiled serenely, stirring in spoon after spoon of sugar.

"I shouldn't worry about that. Viola and I can manage the subterfuge. So long as I know I have your full approval and consent..."

"You do."

"... then I shall go ahead. You can count on me, Margaret." Lady Harriet lifted the steaming cup to her lips, smiling. "I shall secure your son for you. He'll be married to my Viola before the year is out, you can count on that."

***

Margaret tapped on Ewan's study door and waited.

She knew how he hated it when she entered a room without knocking, but really, she was his mother. She had the right to enter without knocking.

Now, though, she needed to be on her best behaviour.

"Come in."

"It's me, dearest." Margaret peeped around the door. Ewan was leaning over some papers on the desk, pen poised in his hands.

"Oh, hello, Mother. Shall I ring for tea?"

"No, nothing like that." Margaret stepped inside, closing the door behind her. "I came to apologize for all that unpleasantness this morning. I don't know what I was thinking."

Ewan's expression softened. "It's alright, Mother. I couldn't disappoint Lucas; you must see that."

Margaret nodded. "Of course, of course. I'm glad you stood your ground."

"Is Lady Harriet very offended?"

"I doubt it. You can talk to her at dinner, though."

"Ah, about that." Ewan winced. "I'm not staying to dinner."

Margaret swallowed past a knot of panic in her throat. "Not staying to dinner? Whyever not?"

"Robert is back in town. I told you, Mother. I've arranged to dine with him in the club tonight. I'm sure I told you."

Margaret opened her mouth to argue, then closed it again. More flies were caught with honey than with vinegar, after all. Berating Ewan and demanding that he spend time with Viola was not going to get anybody anywhere.

"Very well, dearest. It is a pity, though."

Ewan tilted his head to one side. "You really don't mind?"

"Of course not, darling. So long as you are happy. However, would you mind popping into the parlour before you go out, just to say good day to Lady Harriet and Miss Viola?"

Ewan nodded. "Of course I will, Mother. Anything else?"

"Yes, actually." Margaret said, pressing her advantage. "I'd like us to take a trip out to Hyde Park soon. All of us, Ewan. That means you."

He smiled wryly. "Very well. That's quite fair, Mother."

"So, you'll come? No last-minute engagements or vital work emergencies?"

Ewan gave a short laugh. "You don't have a great deal of faith in me, I think. That's fair, I suppose. I promise I will come to Hyde Park. I shall be civil to Lady Harriet, and I shall even be pleasant to Miss Viola."

Margaret brightened. This was progress. It wasn't ideal to know that Ewan wasn't coming to dinner, but really, how much conversation could be had around all that food? She was careful not to show too much of her glee.

"I'm delighted to hear that, Ewan. You know, I think you may find that Miss Viola is a very sweet girl, and a very interesting one. And she is so remarkably beautiful."

Ewan shrugged. "Looks aren't everything, Mother."

That was less encouraging, but Margaret decided to leave it there.

Chapter Seventeen

"I take it you enjoyed the Royal Menagerie and the Tower, your Grace?" Sixsmith asked serenely, making minute adjustments to Ewan's cravat.

Ewan smiled grimly. "I don't think I've had so much fun in years."

Sixsmith paused, narrowing his eyes. "You say it like that is a bad thing, your Grace."

"It is, when that fun is being had with one's own child, a nursemaid, and a governess."

"Ah."

Sixsmith tactfully let the subject drop, and Ewan was grateful. His mind had been buzzing all afternoon.

He'd never been so aware of a person's presence as he was of Hope's.

Not even Caroline's.

Stop it! Ewan scolded himself. He slid his hand into his pocket, feeling the outline of Caroline's miniature. He knew the picture off by heart, without needing to look at it. Her sweet smile, her gentle eyes, her smooth hair. Love had bloomed slowly between him and Caroline. She was a quiet, kind sort of woman, the type that went unnoticed in a busy ballroom. Once Ewan had seen her qualities, however, he hadn't been able to stop looking. They'd been good for each other.

Perfect, in fact.

But Lucas needed a mother.

Oh, Ewan knew of gentlemen who'd been raised without a mother. Whether that meant their mother was literally gone, or whether she simply didn't care, varied. Either way, Ewan saw their flaws, and was determined that his own son would have something of a mother-figure. He'd hoped that his own mother or even Emily could fill that gap, but it was clear that it wasn't working.

The thought which had hovered at the back of Ewan's mind for a while was now becoming more solid, more serious.

I need to marry again. Lucas needs a mother.

The next obvious question, assuming that Ewan could bring himself to seriously contemplate marriage, was who? Who should be marry? The idea of marrying a naïve debutante with her hair full of gowns and parties did not appeal. Besides, what sort of mother would she be? And what if the woman he decided on did not want to be a mother to someone else's child? What then?

And, of course, there was the problem of Hope Barlow.

Namely, whenever Ewan imagined himself marrying someone, or somebody being a mother to Lucas, he imagined Hope.

That was not a good sign. Not at all.

Ewan groaned aloud, shaking his head. "It's too complicated, Sixsmith."

"The cravat, your Grace? I can do a simpler style if you would prefer."

***

Ewan hovered before the parlour door, gathering courage. He could hear the low-level murmur of genteel conversation within. He toyed with the idea of breaking his word to his mother and simply leaving to meet Robert, but of course that wouldn't do. He had promised.

Tapping on the door, Ewan poked his head around.

"Evening, ladies."

There was a chorus of welcome, and Ewan forced himself to step inside and take a seat. This time, there were more seats available, and he wasn't obliged to sit beside Miss Viola.

Perhaps Mother has gotten the message, Ewan thought, beginning to relax.

"How was the Menagerie, then?" Viola asked, leaning forward with a coy smile. "I want to hear everything."

Immediately, Margaret and Lady Harriet resumed their quiet conversation, leaving Ewan with only Viola to talk to.

"That would take a long time, I'm afraid. We enjoyed ourselves very much, though."

Viola nodded, leaning back in her seat. "Will little Lucas be joining us for dinner? I know that you are going out, of course."

"No, it's too late for him. He'll eat his supper with his nursemaid and governess, and then go to bed."

Viola pouted. "What a pity. I do so adore children, you know.

I was hoping to spend more time getting to know him. Your dear Mama has told us so much about him, we were both thrilled to meet little Lucas."

Ewan couldn't hide a smile at that. "He is a sweet boy. He's so kind, so lovely. I truly am blessed. You shall meet him properly someday, Miss Viola."

She tilted her head to one side. "Is that a promise?"

"It certainly is."

"Then I shall hold you to it."

Ewan's gaze wandered to the clock, and he winced.

"I beg your pardon, but I really must be going."

"So soon?" Viola said, disappointed.

"I'm afraid so. Goodnight, everyone. Goodnight, Mother." Ewan bent down to kiss his mother's cheek, and darted out of the door before they could think of another excuse to keep him there.

***

At this time of day, White's was packed, of course.

Ewan forced his way through the mess, trying to keep a genial look on his face. He didn't particularly enjoy clubs, but it was essential that a gentleman – especially a duke – should be clubbable. By that, it meant he had to be good-natured, rich, and important enough to merit membership in at least one 'acceptable' club.

So, that meant that Ewan had to show his face at White's a few times a month.

"Ewan!" came a familiar voice. "There you are! Fashionably late, I see! Over here, I got us seats."

"Hello, Robert." Ewan said, breaking into a smile.

Lord Robert Ashbury was twenty-eight years old, a short, mousy-blond, round-faced man with freckles and a pair of astoundingly beautiful blue-green eyes, flecked with gold. He was the heir to a colossal fortune – besides his own, of course – and various titles from various relatives. He and Ewan were good friends and had been for some time.

He also had a habit of drinking too much too quickly. He was known to be a gentleman who could not imbibe alcohol without adverse consequences, and Ewan had seen him in his cups more times than he could count.

Still, he liked Robert, and so did everyone else.

"Sit down, sit down, my old friend." Robert said, vigorously patting the seat beside him. "I can't wait to hear what's been happening with you. How's little Lucas? Still pining after his godfather?"

Ewan laughed. "I'm sorry to tell you that Lucas doesn't miss you as much as you think. He'll be glad to see you, though, if you want to come for dinner some evening."

"I might just do that, old friend."

Ewan picked up the glass of brandy that Robert had set out for him and took a deep sip. He sat back with a sigh of pleasure and felt himself begin to relax. The noise and the crowd faded into the background, like the buzz of a distant insect.

"So, why aren't you married yet?" Ewan said, after the comfortable silence had dragged on for a while. "Why haven't any of those enthusiastic young debutantes caught you yet?"

Robert grimaced. "They couldn't run fast enough to catch me."

"Oh, ha-ha."

"Yes, ha-ha. But in all seriousness, I haven't met a woman who I felt I could truly love. That's what I want, you see. A love match. It's driving my parents wild."

"I can imagine." Ewan chuckled. He paused before asking his next question. "Did you ever hear anything about the Barlow family? I'm not in Society as much as my mother would like."

Robert pursed his lips. "Barlow? Well, let me see. All I can think of is Viscount Barlow, a silly old rake who gambled away his fortune. Why do you ask?"

Ewan bit his lip, imagining how the conversation would play out. He'd have to explain about Hope, and then Robert would want to know details, and probably would tell other people. He was fond of Robert, but when the man was in his cups, he would divulge all sorts of secrets.

"It doesn't matter." Ewan said lightly. "Just an old friend."

Robert narrowed his eyes, not entirely convinced. "Hm. I see. Well, what's latest with you, then?"

"My mother, in a fit of misguided hospitality, invited Lady Harriet Emsworth and Miss Viola Emsworth to stay. No end date to their stay has been decided on yet."

Ewan had intended that as a light-hearted remark, something to make Robert laugh. He was a little surprised when Robert frowned, setting down his brandy.

"Oh. That's not good. What's brought that on, then?"

"What do you mean?"

Robert glanced around, nibbling his lower lip. "Well, why are they invited?"

"Mother invited them, as I said. Lady Harriet is her friend."

"I'm not sure that anyone is friends with Lady Harriet. She's a scheming sort of person, and too damn clever for her own good. As for her daughter..."

"What's wrong with Miss Viola?"

Robert stopped dead, shooting a quick calculating glance at him. "Why, are you fond of her? Because if you are, I'll stop talking about this right now."

"I am not fond of her. The girl is insufferable. She is my guest, no matter how unwillingly, so I do need to see her sometime, but I'm looking forward to when they leave."

Robert sighed, shaking his head.

"Well, you know how some ladies take the marriage mart a little seriously? Not their faults, of course, the whole thing is set up like a ridiculous competition. Well, I remember Viola Emsworth quite well. She was..." Robert paused, floundering for the right word. "Determined." He finished.

"Determined to find a husband?"

"Not just any husband. The best. The catch of the Season, whoever that was." Robert said grimly. "She's a beautiful girl, and a rich one. There were gentlemen who would have wanted to marry her, but she had her eye on the prize. The first Season, I think it was the young Duke of Kensington – you know, that pimply, red-headed youth?"

"I recall."

"Well, she and her awful mother made a play for him. It didn't work, he married that other girl, that debutante, the name escapes me. Well, they'd spent the whole Season chasing him. After all, he was one of the richest men in England at the time and had about a dozen titles to his name already. Next Season, the Emsworth family panicked. I heard a rumour – and it is just a rumour, mind you – that Lady Harriet conspired with somebody's butler to leave Miss Viola and a gentleman alone together, obviously hoping there'd be a scandal and he'd be forced to marry her."

"Good heavens." Ewan said, a pang of fear going through him. And this woman and her daughter were staying in his house.

"Just a rumour." Robert said firmly. "If it's not true, I'd hate to be talking about it."

"But you think it is true?"

Robert gave a one-shouldered shrug. "Lady Harriet is determined to get a man for her daughter. A catch. It's not enough for her to marry a suitable man, or even somebody she loves. He has to be rich, titled, handsome, and powerful. He has to be somebody. I think Lady Harriet half-heartedly cast her eye on me for Miss Viola last Season, but they decided I wasn't worth the trouble, thank goodness. You know what a fool I can be, blundering around. I'd wake up one morning to find I'd somehow gotten engaged to the girl, and then that's that. Gentlemen like us can't call off engagements."

A shiver ran down Ewan's spine. "I wonder if my mother knows about this."

Robert eyed him for a long moment, his expression unreadable.

"Did... did you think about marrying again, Ewan? It's been a while since Caroline... ahem. Since Caroline. She wouldn't like to think of you being so lonely."

"I'm not lonely." Ewan snapped, with more venom than he'd meant. "Why do people keep thinking that I'm lonely? I don't wish to be impolite, Robert, but I don't need your advice."

Robert blinked, dropping his gaze. "Of course, of course. I'm sorry."

He made a grab for his brandy, lifting it to his lips in a sloppy gulp. Ewan swallowed hard, closing his eyes.

"I'm sorry, Robert. I should never have..."

"I shouldn't have mentioned Caroline."

"No, I shouldn't have spoken to you like that. You are my friend, and if you can't give me advice, who can? Do forgive me."

Robert smiled at that, shaking his head. "Of course I forgive you, you fool."

"It's just… well, I have been thinking that perhaps Lucas needs a mother."

Robert rolled his eyes. "I'm sure he does, but that's not the only reason you should have to get married."

"Well, it's the most important one."

"No, it certainly is not. You deserve love, Ewan. I know you had great affection for Caroline, and you deserve real companionship."

Ewan bit his lip, swallowing past a lump in his throat. He stared into the amber depths of his brandy, willing himself to drink.

"I just don't want to find myself trapped in an engagement to Viola Emsworth." He admitted. "If I do marry again, I want it to be on my own terms. Not that I am considering it, you understand? It's just… just a vague idea."

Robert nodded, passing no comment.

Ewan picked up his brandy glass and drained it with a satisfied sigh.

They sat there for a moment or two in companionable silence, while chatter and laughter rose up around them. Ewan found himself wondering what Hope was doing right now. Probably eating her supper with Lucas, and probably Emily.

Or perhaps Emily had already eaten with Lucas, and Hope was dining alone in her room.

For some reason, this thought sent a pang of sorrow through his chest. Was she lonely? Did she feel isolated, cut adrift from everyone else?

Just like me, Ewan thought.

His thoughts were interrupted by Robert clapping a hand onto his shoulder, making him jump.

"I don't know what you're thinking, but you look sad." He said briskly. "I shall fetch us another drink, and perhaps a bite to eat. You, my dear friend, can sit here and think yourself into a good humour."

Ewan smiled weakly. "Whatever ever you say, old friend. Whatever you say."

Chapter Eighteen

Hope chose a discreet dark-grey gown for that day. She eyed her reflection with resignation. This was as good as it was going to get. Long gone were the days when she could decorate herself with silks and satins or add jewelry and hair-decorations. There was no leisure for trying out new hairstyles that might suit her better, because she had nobody to help her with them. She had to be content with a simple knot, and a plain, dull dress.

She couldn't even allow herself the luxury of vibrant colours these days, because that wouldn't be seemly for a governess.

Enough of such thoughts, Hope reprimanded herself. This is your current reality, and there is no purpose in resisting and lamenting, is there?

Decided, she purposefully turned her back on her own reflection and hurried out of her room.

She had a vague memory of gentlemen turning their heads to watch her as she swept down a hallway, through a crowded ballroom. Their attention was superficial, of course, but it meant so much more. It meant that she was a beautiful, fashionable, interesting young woman, somebody worth looking at. Now, nobody looked twice at her as she went by.

Certainly not Ewan. Why would he bother? Noticing Hope would be like paying attention to a peahen in a crowd of bright, colourful parrots.

Swallowing down a sudden burst of misery, Hope stepped into the schoolroom, putting on a bright smile just in time. Lucas, already sitting at his desk with his feet swinging, beamed at her.

"There you are, Miss Barlow! We're going to Hyde Park today."

Hope blinked. "Hyde Park? I haven't heard anything about that."

Emily, arms full of books, turned from her task of rearranging the bookshelves with an apologetic smile.

"Their Graces decided on it this morning. The guests are coming, too. Lucas is to come, and so are you and I."

"Oh. I see. Well, I'd prepared a history lesson for Lucas today. It's all about our trip to the Tower and the Royal Menagerie.

I spent a great deal of time on it."

Emily loaded the last of the books back onto the shelves and dusted off her hands. She moved close to Hope, dropping her voice so Lucas could not overhear.

"Listen, I'm sure it's not ideal for you at this moment but trust me – it's best to go along with what the family wants. I'm sure you can do the history lesson later, and then do another lesson about the trip to Hyde Park."

"Master Lucas does seem excited." Hope sighed. "I think I'm just in a short mood this morning, I'm not sure why."

That wasn't entirely true. She did know why, and it was all to do with her childhood friend who was probably chatting and flirting with his pretty guest even now.

Hope gave her head a little shake, warning herself against such nonsense. She was here to work, nothing else. She and Ewan were no longer friends, not like they had once been.

"Well, your mood is about to get a lot worse." Emily said, wincing. "Her Grace, the Dowager wants to see you. In her private parlour."

Margaret? Margaret wanted to see her? Hope swallowed hard, her throat closing up.

"I don't suppose there's the slightest chance that it's good news?" Hope sighed.

Emily pulled a face. "I doubt it. She said that I should tell you as soon as you arrived in the schoolroom or nursery. So, I'm telling you now. I wouldn't keep her waiting, if I were you."

"I should go now, I suppose." Hope said reluctantly. "I'll be back in a minute, Master Lucas."

She slipped out of the schoolroom and strode purposefully down the hallway. No doubt the Dowager had something to scold her about, or perhaps she'd finally found an excuse to dismiss her. Either way, Hope was keen to get it over with.

She rounded a corner, head full of her own thoughts, and nearly collided head-on with the Duke himself.

"Carefully there, Miss Barlow!" Ewan said, laughing.

Hope flushed, mumbling an apology and making to step around him. She almost forgot to dip a curtsey, making a quick, lopsided bow at the last minute.

"Wait a moment." Ewan said.

Hope stopped dead. She wished that her heart would stop pounding so furiously. She felt as though she might explode. Ewan's hand stretched out to stop her leaving, but his fingers only grazed the side of her arm. She could feel his touch like nothing else, heat tingling along her skin. She turned reluctantly to face him.

Ewan eyed her for a long moment, nibbling his lower lip. "What's the matter? You seem preoccupied."

Hope forced a smile. "Nothing is the matter. Did you need my help, your Grace?"

Ewan gave a light chuckle. "You know, I'll never quite get used to hearing you call me 'Your Grace'. Didn't you win every single fencing match we had, back when we only had wooden twigs for swords?"

Hope smiled despite herself, remembering their long treks into the woods in search of perfect swords, and their lengthy, intrigue-ridden battles.

"I did win, didn't I?"

"On our outing to the Menagerie and the Tower, it almost felt like old times again. Didn't you think so?"

"I did." Hope admitted, before she could think twice about the wisdom of saying such a thing. Ewan beamed, and his smile made something warm and tingling bloom in her chest.

"I'm glad, Hope. I am glad. That's what I came to tell you today – I enjoyed your company, and I'd like to repeat our outing again sometime. Lucas had a wonderful time too – he hasn't stopped talking about it."

"I'm so pleased he enjoyed himself. He is such a sweet boy, and real pleasure to teach."

Ewan smiled wider, clearly pleased at the compliment to his son.

"I thought we could spend some time planning outings now, if you like. Unless you have somewhere to be, of course?"

"I... I actually have to meet her Grace the Dowager in her private parlour as soon as possible."

Ewan blinked, missing a beat. "Oh. I wasn't aware that Mother had set up a meeting with you."

"I only heard of it this morning." Hope eyed Ewan's face, noting a touch of suspicion on his face. What did he think his mother was going to do?

"It'll just be about Lucas' education, I'm sure." Ewan said, almost as if he were trying to convince himself. "I shall go with you."

Just like that, the stone of dread in Hope's stomach disappeared, like a knot of sand disintegrating under the force of a wave. If Ewan was there, Margaret couldn't really hurt her, could she? Besides, as the Duke and Lucas' father, Ewan had every right to attend such a meeting.

"That would be nice, thank you." Hope said, hoping that she didn't seem too relieved. "I am going there now."

"Well, let's not keep my mother waiting – she's not the most patient of women."

Hope tapped on the closed door to Margaret's private parlour and waited. Ewan stayed silent.

"Who is it?" came the Dowager's austere tones from within.

"It is Miss Barlow, your Grace."

"Ah, Miss Barlow. I expected you a little sooner, but no matter. Come in."

Hope did so, pushing open the door. The Dowager had her back to the doorway, leaning over her writing desk. She turned, not hurrying, with a bright smile on her face.

Ewan stepped into the parlour behind Hope, and the smile dropped off the Dowager's face like a stone. The look she gave Hope was nothing short of an accusation.

Not a wonderful start, Hope thought.

Chapter Nineteen

Margaret resisted the urge to fling a paperweight at the girl's head.

What was she thinking, towing Ewan along behind her? It had all been arranged – Margaret would have a quiet word with Miss Barlow and get her out of the way for today at least, and all would be fine. But now that Ewan had come tagging along with her, she would have to tread more carefully.

She realized with a spike of annoyance that the muffled, cheerful voices she'd heard from further down the hallway must have been Ewan and Miss Barlow conversing with each other.

"What are you doing here, Ewan?" Margaret said, before she could stop herself. She immediately saw her son's eyes narrow in suspicion. He probably thought she was going to try and sneakily fire the girl.

Don't tempt me, Margaret thought.

"Miss Barlow said that you'd summoned her to a private meeting. I assumed that it concerned Lucas' education, so I thought I'd better be present."

Margaret flashed a quick smile, revealing no teeth. "I wasn't aware that Miss Barlow went running to you with updates on everything I requested of her. How long has that been going on?"

Miss Barlow, the scheming harpy, had the grace to blush. Ewan, on the other hand, scowled.

"Don't be unkind, Mother. Miss Barlow does nothing of the sort. I happened to meet her, and asked if she would help me plan outings for Lucas. She couldn't do so right away, as she was meeting you. She neither went out of her way to tell me about this, but neither did she conceal it."

Margaret pursed her lips, aware that she was starting to look bad-tempered and ungracious. She picked non-existent bits of fluff off her skirts and pasted on the Society smile she reserved for guests that had well outstayed their welcome.

"Of course, of course. I meant no harm. Speaking of outings, Miss Barlow, I summoned you here because I have some rather good news, which I think you'll like very much." She paused for a moment, allowing the tension to build just a little. "You may have heard that we are going on a trip to Hyde Park for a picnic."

"I did hear, your Grace." Miss Barlow said, eyes modestly levelled downwards. "I wasn't aware until this morning. Master Lucas' history lesson will need to be postponed."

Margaret snorted. "Yes, it certainly will. Since we are all going on an outing, I have brought you here to inform you that you may take the rest of the day as a holiday."

She leaned back, smiling magnanimously. Margaret had spent long and hard thinking about how to get Miss Barlow out of the way for an outing, and unfortunately a holiday was all she could think of. It wouldn't be too inconvenient. Emily would mind Lucas, and she and Lady Harriet would chat, leaving Ewan free to talk to Miss Viola. Well, he'd have to talk to her.

She waited in vain for gratitude, for smiles and thank yous. Miss Barlow blinked, missing a beat.

"Oh, I see. Very well, your Grace."

"Very well?" Margaret echoed waspishly. "I give you a holiday, and all you say is very well? You ought to work on your gratitude, my girl."

"I beg your pardon." Hope said, at the same instant that Ewan said, "Mother!"

Margaret forced herself to compose her emotions. It was irritating that Ewan had accompanied the girl in here. If it had just been her and Miss Barlow, she would have announced Miss Barlow's unwanted and unasked for holiday without caring what she thought about it or not. Miss Barlow would probably go out, and then it would be done. They could enjoy her day, without that dreadful governess three steps behind them. Margaret could swear that she was always listening and judging.

That was the sort of audacity she had left behind when they became Nobility. Margaret would never go back to hiring bored, disrespectful servants who cared nothing for title or good breeding. She was a duchess now – or a dowager, rather – and her subordinates would not forget it.

Not even the governesses.

She straightened her back a little. "Miss Barlow, you don't seem pleased about your holiday."

"It's not that, your Grace." Miss Barlow said, humbly enough to fool anyone. "I just wasn't expecting it."

Margaret sniffed, adjusting her skirts. "Well, that's hardly the point. As I said, we are going out to Hyde Park, and there will be no need for your services today. Once we return, Emily will of course attend to Master Lucas."

"Well, why doesn't Miss Barlow come with us to Hyde Park?" Ewan said.

Margaret's blood ran cold.

No, no, no! This wasn't what was meant to happen! This wasn't right at all!

"I have just told Miss Barlow that she can have a holiday, and that there is no need of her services." Margaret said testily, willing Miss Barlow to come up with some excuse or a polite refusal.

"I wouldn't want to intrude." Miss Barlow said. To Margaret's rage, she addressed the comment to Ewan, rather than her.

"You aren't intruding." Ewan said eagerly, so eagerly that Margaret wanted to slap him and remind him of who he was. And more to the point, who she wasn't.

He's letting down his guard, Margaret thought, with a flash of impotent rage.

"It'll work out well, I think. Since Miss Barlow is on holiday, she can accompany us and simply enjoy herself. Lucas would love to see you there; I know he would."

Margaret swallowed hard. "I'm sure Miss Barlow has other things to do than follow us around Hyde Park, Ewan. Do stop pressuring her."

It was a little, too late. Miss Barlow was looking at Ewan, with a misty look in her eyes that Margaret did not like, not one bit.

"I should like to come, if it's not too much trouble." She said, her voice soft and her gaze fixed on Ewan.

He smiled, a wide, toothy grin that Margaret hadn't seen for far too long, and it irked her that Hope Barlow was the one to bring it to the surface again.

"Excellent! It's all settled. There, you see, Mother? No need for you to worry. Now, Miss Barlow, if you have a minute, we could plan some other outings for Lucas, perhaps later this month. You mentioned that you had a plan for history today, based on our trip to the Tower and the Menagerie? I'd love to take a look at them."

Miss Barlow beamed. "Oh, certainly. I had some ideas for outings that Master Lucas would enjoy. Did you wish to speak to me further, your Grace?"

Now she was looking at Margaret, already half-turned towards the door. Margaret racked her brains for something to keep her there, something to scold her about, but the girl was wretchedly good at her job, and besides, Ewan would stay, too.

If I hadn't given her that wretched holiday, she would at least have had to busy herself with taking care of Lucas, Margaret thought bitterly.

She pressed her lips together and forced a smile.

"Nothing that I can think of."

"Good, that's good." Ewan said, with more than a hint of relief. "Shall we take tea in the schoolroom while we talk, Miss Barlow?"

"I should like that, thank you."

And then the two of them left, closing the door softly behind them. Margaret stayed where she was, fuming. The blasted girl had barely given her a curtsey when she left. Of course, she had curtsied, but it wasn't a very deep or meaningful one.

This was trouble, Margaret could tell. Ewan wasn't keeping his distance from the girl. They were running into each other far too often, getting more comfortable in each other's presence and, doubtless, reminiscing over old times.

Fatal.

If she didn't intervene now, Ewan might forget how far below him was Miss Hope Barlow, and she in turn might start to believe that Ewan – a duke – was within her reach.

No, something had to be done. Margaret scrambled to her feet, diving across to the bell at the corner of the room. She hauled on it and then paced angrily in front of the fireplace until the door opened and a footman stood there. She barely looked at the man.

"Fetch Miss Viola and Lady Harriet." Margaret said brusquely. "I daresay they'll have a dozen excuses as to why they can't come here, but you're to bring them here, to me, as soon as possible, do you understand? It's extremely urgent. Now, go."

The poor footman murmured something polite and obedient, then left. The minutes felt like hours, and Margaret's nerves were stretched to the limit as she waited.

Finally, finally, she heard Lady Harriet's heavy tread approaching along the hallway, followed by Miss Viola's mincing steps.

They slipped inside, closing the door behind them.

"I don't appreciate being summoned to your rooms like a naughty child, Margaret." Lady Harriet said heavily. "Viola was in the middle of her toilette."

Margaret barely spared Viola a second glance. "That governess is coming with us today."

Lady Harriet blinked. "I thought you intended to give her the day off."

"I did, I did. I gave her the day off, then my foolish son invited her to come along with us."

"Why would he invite her to come with us?" Viola questioned, wrinkling her tiny, pretty nose. "She's a governess. It's bad enough that we have to bring that silly little boy…"

"That is my grandson." Margaret snapped. "And if you want to get anywhere at all with my son, you'd better dote on him."

Lady Harriet gave her daughter a level look, and Viola blushed, dropping her gaze.

"Viola, go and finish getting ready. We'll talk in here."

Visibly pleased to be released, Viola got to her feet and skipped out. Or rather, she tried to skip, but her fashionably heeled shoes didn't quite allow for it.

Margaret let out a sigh of relief once the girl was gone.

"I hope I'm not making a mistake." She said, half to herself, eyeing the door. "Viola is very pretty, but I want the right kind of daughter-in-law. Caroline was very dear to me, you know."

Lady Harriet snorted, settling herself deeper into the sofa she'd chosen.

"Well, it sounds to me like your options are my Viola, or the governess. Which would you prefer."

Margaret blanched. "I beseech you, do not jest about such matters."

"I assure you, I am not jesting. It appears to me that the Duke has taken a liking to the young miss. Perhaps it would have been prudent to engage a governess of more advanced years."

"Do you think I don't know that, Harriet? None of this would be a problem if they weren't old friends."

"That certainly complicates matters. Only for you, of course. Viola can go back into Society and snatch up a prize in no time. The Duke, of course, would be a preferable match, but if he is sifting through the refuse collection for a suitable spouse, then..."

"Be careful, Harriet." Margaret said, bristling. "We both know that Viola is not the roaring success in Society you hoped she would be. She'd make a fine daughter-in-law for me, I'm sure, but it is up to her to prove herself. Ewan needs... well, he just needs a little encouragement. That's why I needed the governess out of the way, so he can concentrate on Viola. I'm sure that once he sees her charms, he'll realize just how below him the governess is. Not that he's thinking seriously about her, of course. He would never stoop to such a thing."

Lady Harriet's face remained bland and placid as always. Margaret wasn't fooled. She'd learned a long time ago that still waters run deep, and Lady Harriet was no exception. She was a woman who was always thinking, always planning. Always prepared.

"I shouldn't worry too much." She said eventually. "A duke and a governess? It's the stuff of novels, and no person of sense would think of it. Frankly, I doubt that Miss Barlow has the audacity to raise her eyes to the Duke, regardless of their history. And I am sure that he, in turn, knows what is expected of him and how he should behave."

"But will he turn his eye to Viola? That is what worries me."

"Yes." Lady Harriet said, almost without pause. "Yes, I think he will. It's not ideal that the governess is coming along today, but perhaps it will do him good to compare her to Viola. Men are fickle things, and he'll quickly see the governess' flaws. I shall instruct Viola to be especially obliging and charming to the Duke today. You and I shall conspire to keep him and the governess apart. Is there no pretext you could use to dismiss her?"

"None." Margaret remarked miserably. "She's clever, conscientious, and Lucas adores her already. The servants like her, and more to the point, Ewan likes her."

Lady Harriet grunted, heaving herself to her feet. "Then she'll be a formidable opponent. Not to worry, though. Fear not, Margaret, for I shall handle her with ease. Just trust in my

guidance, and all shall be well."
> Margaret drummed her fingers on her knee.
> I wish I could believe you, she thought.

Chapter Twenty

"And Miss Barlow is definitely coming with us?" Lucas said, shifting from foot to foot while his father buttoned his jacket. Emily hovered in the background, a scarf and a pair of mittens clutched to her chest.

"She certainly is." Ewan replied, smiling.

"I'm glad. I like Miss Barlow."

"So do I. You know, Miss Barlow and I used to go on picnics like this when we were barely older than you."

Lucas perked up at this. "Really? In Hyde Park?"

"I don't remember the locations, but places like that, yes. Places with lots of trees and woodland, and lots of little streams running everywhere. We'd play hide-and-seek, and Tag, and all kinds of pretend games. It was like I had a little sister of my own."

"I would like a little sister." Lucas said contemplatively. "Papa, can I have a little sister?"

Ewan winced. "I can't promise anything, and you'll certainly have to wait for a while."

Lucas seemed disappointed but accepted it.

"If you and Miss Barlow are friends, why didn't I see her before she came here to be my governess?"

Ewan hesitated. That was a very good question, and one that couldn't be answered easily.

"I suppose we grew apart." He said, after a moment or two.

"What does that mean?"

"It means that our lives started to be different. We didn't have as much time to spend together, and so on. Of course, me and your Grandmama moved somewhere else, and my father ended up becoming a duke. We didn't see Miss Barlow at all after that."

"Why not?" Came the inevitable reply.

Ewan sighed, sitting back on his heels to inspect Lucas' clothing.

"I think he'll need the scarf, Emily, it is chilly out there today."

Emily darted forward, draping the scarf around Lucas' neck. Ewan began to adjust it.

"To answer your question," he continued, "We were simply too far away. And by then, I think, we didn't move in the same circles. That is, we didn't really have the same friends anymore."

Lucas tilted his head to one side. "Does that make a difference?"

Ewan raked a hand through his hair. "I suppose it shouldn't, but yes, it does. Now. Enough questions for today, eh? You're giving your old Papa a headache."

"I won't ask any more questions." Lucas said obediently. "Unless I think of more questions I want to ask later on."

Ewan laughed. "That's fair."

He was suddenly aware of Emily standing behind him, very still and intent. When he glanced her way, she was looking at him, a curious expression on her face. She immediately dropped her gaze when she caught his eye, but it was too late.

I ought to be more careful, Ewan thought grimly. Ridiculous as these rules are, a duke is not meant to be friends with a governess. I'm lucky that Emily doesn't gossip, or it would be all over the town that the Duke of Darenwood is close, personal friends with a common governess.

He immediately felt guilty for thinking of Hope as a common governess. Perhaps Margaret's aspirations had finally gotten to him.

Pushing aside the thought, Ewan got to his feet, extending his hand to Lucas.

"Come along, let's go downstairs. It's time to leave."

With the conversation already forgotten, Lucas bounced along beside Ewan, chattering nonstop about where he wanted to go and what he wanted to do. He was particularly intrigued by the games Ewan had played when he was a child, and Ewan spent the rest of the trip downstairs telling his son about the epic battles – armed with wooden sticks – that he and Hope Barlow had fought with each other.

Halfway down the stairs, he heard the unmistakable peal of Society laughter, and some of Ewan's good humour ebbed away.

They'd all gathered in the foyer downstairs. The front door stood open, letting in a cool blast of air, and Ewan spotted the two carriages he'd ordered for today to take them all to Hyde Park.

Lady Harriet had taken a seat in the foyer, and sat in silence, her eyes glittering, darting to and fro and missing nothing. Margaret seemed on edge, barely listening to Miss Viola's chatter.

Miss Viola had chosen a vibrant yellow silk dress, adorned with red ribbons and red rosettes, and had her hair done up in a tremendous style, all ringlets and carefully arranged curls.

She looked marvellous, but Ewan couldn't help but wonder whether that colour of gown was ideal for a picnic. Grass stains would never come out of that silk. What was more, the brisk wind would undo the hours of work put into her hair.

Still, it was none of his concern what Miss Viola wanted to wear. With Robert's warning ringing in his ears, Ewan descended the last few steps, and Margaret darted forward to greet him.

"See, Viola, Lucas is coming along with us!" Margaret exclaimed, glancing back at the young woman.

Drawing in a deep, fortifying breath, Viola dived forward, arms out.

"Hello, my sweet boy!" she cooed, advancing on Lucas. "What a darling little creature you are! Look at your little cheeks! Come and give me a hug."

Lucas drew back, clutching Ewan's hand, and buried his face in the side of his father's leg.

Viola blinked, disconcerted, and let her arms drop to her sides.

"He isn't very friendly." She remarked.

"He's young." Ewan explained, sheltering Lucas protectively. "He's very excited for our picnic today. Lucas, perhaps you might make Miss Viola a daisy chain?"

Lucas peeped out, a hint of a smile on his face.

"A little boy? Make a daisy chain? How silly!" Viola laughed.

Lucas hid his face again.

"Master Lucas is very clever at making things like that." Came a familiar voice.

Hope Barlow stepped out from a shadowy corner, where she'd been standing, unnoticed, for goodness only knew how long.

Lucas beamed, releasing Ewan's hand and darting over to her.

"Miss Barlow, Miss Barlow! I'm so pleased you're coming with us!" he cried, holding up his arms.

Hope lifted him up, smiling, and Ewan found himself

transfixed.

"You changed your gown." He said, before he could stop himself. He could almost feel Margaret's gaze boring into his face.

Hope smiled weakly, smoothing out her pale-blue skirts. "I brought it for a special occasion. Since today is a day off, I thought I ought to wear it."

"It suits you."

She went red, dropping her gaze. "Thank you, your Grace."

Ewan remembered himself, turning to face the stony expressions of his mother, Miss Viola, and Lady Harriet.

"Shall we go?" he said brightly.

"Papa, are you and me going in the carriage with Emily and Miss Barlow?" Lucas asked eagerly.

Before Ewan could reply, Margaret chimed in.

"No, no, Lucas! Your Papa and I are riding with Lady Harriet and Miss Viola. Miss Barlow, put Lucas down at once. He can stand on his own feet, thank you very kindly. Lucas, you like Miss Viola, don't you? Isn't she pretty?"

Lucas, with surprising tact for a child of his age, said nothing.

Margaret pursed her lips. "You are coming with us, aren't you, Ewan? I suppose if Lucas wants to go in the carriage with Emily and Miss Barlow, he can, and then you can come with us. There might be more room that way, anyway."

Ewan bit his lip. He was aware that they were all looking at him. Lady Harriet and his mother might be maneuvering things behind the scenes, but the fact remained that he was the man of the house, Lucas' father, and the Duke. He had the final say.

"Lucas, what would you like to do?" he asked eventually.

"Don't you want to go with Miss Viola and me?" Margaret interrupted, crouching down to look him in the eye. She had a peculiar look on her face, as if she were trying to compel him to say something without actually saying so.

Lucas shrank back against Miss Barlow's skirts, glancing up at her for support. Margaret did not like this one bit. Ewan was perfectly placed to see his mother shoot an angry, poisonous look up at the governess. He frowned, trying to catch her eye.

Margaret caught him looking and had the grace to blush. She rose unsteadily to her feet, shaking back her hair with an exaggerated carelessness.

"Well, I suppose if Lucas wants to travel with his governess and nursemaid, there's not a great deal I can do." She said lightly, giving her grandson a look of level disappointment.

Oblivious to his grandmother's disapproval, Lucas beamed up at Miss Barlow. Ewan saw the governess tuck away a tiny smile, and squeeze Lucas' small hand.

Miss Viola was pouting, almost comically so.

"Well, I am disappointed. I thought that you and I could talk, your Grace." She tossed back her glossy ringlets, smiling coyly at him. Ewan swallowed his unease.

"That's very kind of you, Miss Viola. However, we'll all be meeting up in the same place, won't we? It's only a short carriage ride, barely half an hour. Nothing to worry about."

"I'm sure we can rearrange the seating plans on the way back." Lady Harriet said, smiling placidly. "So that everyone is kept happy."

Ewan met her gaze squarely. "Yes. Or we could keep it the same, couldn't we?"

Not wanting to prolong the conversation – which seemed to be a great fuss over nothing, in his opinion – Ewan took Lucas' hand and led the way down to the carriages.

He climbed in easily, hauling Lucas up after him. Emily followed, and Miss Barlow last of all. Since Lucas had spread himself over one seat, and Emily sat down in the remaining space beside him, that meant that Miss Barlow had no choice but to sit directly beside Ewan.

The door closed firmly after them, and they were off.

Chapter Twenty-One

Hope wasn't a fool, and she would have had to be a spectacularly oblivious one to misinterpret the Dowager's behavior. It was obvious that the sudden 'holiday' was nothing more than an excuse to make sure Hope didn't accompany them on the picnic. The Dowager was visibly irritated by Ewan's insistence on her coming.

Really, Hope ought to have politely refused the invitation. But the idea of being so near to Ewan was more tempting than she cared to admit. Besides, they had been getting on so well. And Lucas was so eager for her to come, Hope couldn't have brought herself to disappoint him.

But now she'd made an enemy of the Dowager, and doubtless an enemy of Lady Harriet and Miss Viola too, who both clearly expected Miss Viola to become the Duchess of Darenwood one day soon.

The thought of Miss Viola and Ewan approaching the altar together, arm in arm, sent a pang through Hope. A pang she ought not to be feeling.

Remember your place, Hope told herself, hating the words even as she thought them. Don't get too ambitious – you'll surely be punished for it.

The carriage jolted over a pothole, making her fall against Ewan. His strong frame barely shifted, reaching out an arm to steady her. Scarlet-faced, Hope murmured thanks and pointedly turned her face to the window.

She wished she had gotten in the carriage first. Then she could be sitting beside Lucas right now, helping him read a picture book, instead of spending every instant hyper-aware of the man beside her.

Hope stole a look at Ewan out of the corner of her eye. She'd never imagined that her childhood friend would grow up to be so devastatingly handsome. And yet, she could see traces of the little boy she'd once known.

We were equals then, she thought sadly. Just two children playing together. Nothing more, nothing less.

She cleared her throat, sitting up a little straighter.

"Hope?" Ewan said, his voice low. "Are you alright? Are you feeling sick?"

She blushed. "No, not at all. I'm just... just tired."

She would have to be extremely careful today. Margaret would be watching her like a hawk, and so would Lady Harriet.

Maybe I shouldn't have come, Hope thought miserably.

"Miss Barlow?" Lucas said, wriggling into a sitting position. "Have you ever been to Hyde Park before?"

Hope smiled. "Yes, but many years ago. I expect it's entirely different now."

"I'll show you all my favourite spots." Lucas promised, and Hope felt the urge to wrap her arms around him and hold him close. She contented herself with smiling at him.

"I can't wait for it."

The carriage rolled through the entrance to the Park, and Hope found herself craning her neck to peer out. She really hadn't been to the Park in a while. Apparently, it was still as crowded as ever, despite the chilly day.

Families and clumps of young people milled around, chattering and laughing between themselves, eating ices – ices? In this weather! – and pointing at various attractions. The carriage slowed almost to a stop, carefully wheeling its way through the crowd. A memory stirred, and Hope remembered that soon the paved, wide terraces would give way to woodland and flat, grassy stretches, perfect for a picnic. The crowds thinned as they pushed on through the Park, and the carriages eventually ground to a halt.

She could see a grassy knoll to their left, with a large, leafy oak tree leaning over it all, lopsided and ancient.

"That's where we're going to sit." Ewan said, breath brushing her ear, and Hope shivered. Ewan drew back, as if he hadn't realized that he was leaning so close. Then one of the footmen opened the carriage door, and there was nothing to do but climb out.

Hope drew in deep lungfuls of clean, fresh air, while Emily, Lucas, and Ewan climbed out of the carriage behind her. In the second carriage, just behind them, Lady Harriet was heaving herself down to the ground, the Dowager peeping over her shoulder from inside. Miss Viola was out, and currently was alternatively staring at the grass and her own white satin slippers.

Conscious of being watched, she glanced at Hope. Her pretty face immediately crumpled into a scowl, and she turned away with a toss of her head.

Perhaps she was hoping that I'd fall out of the carriage on the way, Hope thought, with a flash of amusement.

Lady Harriet finally heaved herself free, and the Dowager dropped neatly to the ground behind her. She glanced briefly at Hope then turned away, as if her appearance here did not matter a jot.

"Now," the Dowager said lightly. "Let's get on with it, shall we? We'll have two picnic blankets, one for Lucas, the nursemaid, and the governess, and the second for the rest of us. Now, let's get to it!"

"This is for you." Lucas announced, holding a small posy of wildflowers under Hope's nose. "I was going to make a daisy chain, but Emily said that I would get my hands dirty, and we haven't eaten yet."

"Emily is very wise." Hope said, smiling at the nursemaid. "Thank you, Lucas. These are lovely."

The blankets had indeed been set out under the oak tree. It was a picturesque view, with green fields, nodding wildflowers, and deep woodlands as far as the eye could see. They'd chosen their spot well – from here, they could almost believe that they were the only people in the Park.

The largest blanket held Lady Harriet, Miss Viola, the Dowager, and of course Ewan. It was spread out in the prime spot underneath the oak tree. The blanket that Hope, Emily, and Lucas shared was set on something of an incline, just below the larger blanket. Hope found herself leaning to one side to save herself from sagging sideways, and her drink kept spilling. The food had been arranged on the larger blanket. Of course, Lucas jumped up and down to help himself to whatever he wanted, while Miss Viola cooed over him with an almost convincing adoration.

Emily and Hope would have gone hungry if Ewan hadn't instructed the footman to take the basket over to them, too, ignoring the Dowager's sour expression. Nobody talked to Hope or Emily, of course. Ewan had been carefully positioned on the furthest corner of the blanket, so that there were a full two blankets between Ewan and Hope. She could see Miss Viola nestling against him, the profusion of her yellow silk skirts nearly enveloping them both. She kept tittering at whatever he said, and coyly trying to convince him to eat various sweetmeats.

Lady Harriet and the Dowager kept their conversation strictly between themselves, so that Ewan had no choice but to converse with Miss Viola.

And then their eyes met across the picnic blankets and paraphernalia. Miss Viola was in the middle of a long, convoluted anecdote. Ewan met Hope's eye, and his eyebrow flickered, just a little. Hope hid a smile, and glanced back up to find him smiling, too.

I don't care if Miss Viola sits with him, Hope thought to herself, in a rush of pride. Ewan and I are friends. We'll always be friends, and she can't change that.

Something made her glance up again, and this time it was Lady Harriet staring at her, the woman's expression hard and intent. Hope's good feeling filtered away, leaving her cold.

Slowly and deliberately, Lady Harriet heaved her bulk into a different position, so that she sat directly between Ewan and Hope. Now, Hope couldn't see anything of either Miss Viola or Ewan, except for a few swatches of yellow silk.

"Chin up." Emily said, cutting into Hope's thoughts. She met the nursemaid's eyes, and Emily gave her a lopsided smile. "Come on, have some more lemonade, eh?"

Chapter Twenty-Two

Today was not going at all how Ewan had planned. When Margaret had suggested a picnic in Hyde Park, he'd imagined that he would have his mother on one side of him and his son on the other, with Miss Barlow sitting opposite, smiling at him.

Instead, he found himself all but glued to Miss Viola. She was leaning as close to him as she could without climbing into his lap, and her perfume was almost stifling. The swathes of her slippery yellow dress kept getting in his way, too. Now, Lady Harriet was seated between him and the second picnic blanket. He couldn't even see Hope and Lucas anymore.

It was infuriating, but the chains of propriety and politeness kept Ewan securely in place.

"So, are you looking forward to the ball, your Grace?" Viola asked, fluttering her eyelashes. "You must be positively perishing for some proper Society."

What do you mean, Proper Society? Ewan thought, followed quickly by, *What ball?*

"Ball?" he echoed. "Whose?"

She gave a dainty titter of laughter. "Oh, your Grace, you are so droll. I mean yours, of course. Her Grace, the Dowager told us about it this morning."

Ewan met his mother's eye over the ham sandwiches. She was taking a long sip of her tea, ostensibly trying to avoid notice.

"You're throwing a party, Mother?" Ewan said, trying to sound calm. "Dare I ask where?"

Margaret coughed delicately. "Why, at home, of course. We can't very well host a ball anywhere else."

"I don't recall you asking me."

She stiffened, drawing up. "I didn't realize I had to."

Ewan bit back on his sharp retorts.

Of course you had to. What made you think you didn't?

He took a deep breath, reminding himself once again that his mother was only trying to do what was best. She'd been the mistress of their home for many years, and it wasn't fair to expect her to simply get out of the habit now.

"It doesn't matter." Ewan said carefully. "It's arranged now.

So, a ball, then? When is the great day?"

"You must dance with me, your Grace." Miss Viola said eagerly, riding roughshod over her own mother, who was about to answer Ewan's question. "I'll wager that you are a fine dancer."

Ewan sucked in a breath, a memory coming hurtling back.

Himself and Hope, face to face, serious and quiet in a huge, empty ballroom. He couldn't remember exactly how old he was. Not above twelve, that was for sure.

"I have a dancing master." Hope was saying, her voice young and high-pitched. "He teaches me to dance, and my cousin, too. Mama says that dancing is soothing for the soul, but Papa says that she is silly, and a dancing master is too expensive, and I should enjoy it while I can. Shall I show you?"

"Ewan is an excellent dancer." Margaret cut in eagerly. "I remember when he..." she launched into a comical tale of a young Ewan doing something or other. Ewan stopped listening, lost in his own memories.

"Dancing looks hard." Young Ewan said, subdued. "It looks ever so complicated."

"It's easy." Hope said, with the firm, unearned confidence of youth. "I shall show you. Here, we stand facing each other, like so. We have to hold hands."

"I don't want to hold hands."

"Well, we can pretend to hold hands if you'd prefer, but it is easier if we do it properly." Hope said, endlessly patient.

Ewan shuffled closer, allowing Hope to place one hand on her side and the other in her hand, and she placed her remaining hand on his shoulder.

"Now we step to the side... like so... then this, and this, then that, and around again. You have to twirl me, Ewan. There! That is easy, is it not?"

"It is not easy. My feet won't move like yours."

"Mama says that it takes practice." Hope assured him. "But that it is worth the practice."

"I'll look silly."

Hope pursed her lips. "I don't think you look silly." She said stoutly, nodding for emphasis. "And even if you did, there's nobody in here to see you."

Ewan glanced around at the cavernous ballroom. It was an

odd room to be in when it was empty. There was something about the space that seemed designed to be filled with people. There should be chatter, laughter, music, and general noise. There should be food and drink everywhere, and the air should be stuffy and hot. This echoing emptiness was strange beyond words.

"Very well." Ewan said. "Let's try again."

"Good! I shall count out the beat. One, two, three, four. One, two, three, four. One…"

They twirled round and round the huge ballroom, two tiny children in a vast space designed for grown-ups. Their footsteps echoed, and so did their laughter. They stood on each other's toes, and Ewan often went the wrong way in their turns, and then when he got the hang of it, he went entirely too fast and spun Hope off her feet. They collapsed onto the shiny, polished floor and dissolved into giggles.

Ewan thought that he could almost hear the echoing strains of music in his head.

"Your Grace? Goodness, you are quite distracted!"

Ewan blinked, coming back to the real, present world in an unpleasant rush. He gave his head a little shade, drowning out the faint sound of Hope's childish voice counting out the beats of some unheard music.

Miss Viola, who'd been staring up at him with annoyance when he didn't appear to be listening to her, hastily turned her frown into a teasing smile.

"Did we bore you with our tales of dancing and dresses? With our womanly chatter? Oh, what you must endure, you unfortunate gentleman!"

Ewan smiled weakly.

"The late Duchess was very impressed with my dancing when we first met." He said, not entirely sure where the words had come from.

Miss Viola blinked, glancing over at her mother for clarification.

"Ah, yes, your previous wife." Lady Harriet said, an edge to her voice. "What a tragedy. Still, life goes on, does it not? We cannot let ourselves fall behind. I am sure she would wish you to be happy and fulfilled in your life. In my experience, any good woman would want her dear husband to find love and affection with another fine woman, someone suitable for him. You ought to respect the wishes of your poor, late Duchess, your Grace."

That was pointed. Miss Viola shuffled a little closer to Ewan.

He glanced at his mother, and saw that Margaret had her gaze pointedly averted downwards. If she felt uncomfortable over Lady Harriet's shameless use of poor Caroline as a way to push Ewan towards Miss Viola, she didn't let on.

Ewan was beginning to feel sick. Maybe it was the carriage ride – during which he'd spent the whole time conscious that Hope was sitting right beside him, close enough to touch – or perhaps it was the sweet, sugary food Margaret had packed for the picnic lunch.

"Quite right." Ewan managed, flashing a tight, noncommittal smile at Lady Harriet. He made no attempt to continue the conversation, and an uncomfortable silence descended.

"So, your Grace, you haven't yet answered my question." Miss Viola said lightly, her voice almost imperceptibly strained.

"And what question is that?" Ewan craned his neck, trying to see around Lady Harriet's bulk if Lucas, Emily, and Hope were safe and well. He hadn't heard Lucas' laughter for a while.

"Well, whether you'll dance with me, or not?"

Ewan allowed himself to imagine choosing the second option. He imagined smiling sweetly at Miss Viola and telling her that he would rather kick an iron lamppost than dance with her.

Tempting, but not possible. Instead, he gave another tight, unhappy smile.

"Of course, I should love to dance with you, Miss Viola. Assuming, of course, that your dance card isn't full within moments of the ball starting. I should hate to take you away from other gentlemen."

Was that pointed enough? Lady Harriet's gaze narrowed, but Miss Viola only tittered, obviously assuming that he was paying her a compliment.

"Oh, your Grace, you are so witty I hardly know what to say to you! Of course I shall make room for you on my dance card. We can dance together twice, can we not? Three times would be scandalous for a couple not married, of course." She fluttered her eyelashes up at him, and Ewan tried not to notice.

"Then we had better not dance together three times, then."

He said tightly. Finally peering around Lady Harriet, Ewan noticed with a start that the picnic blanket was empty. The three of them were gone.

It was pointless to ask if anyone else had seen them going. Lady Harriet had her back to them, Margaret was lost in her own private world of worry and possibly shame, and Miss Viola didn't seem to be able to see beyond the end of her own nose.

"But if we dance together twice..." Miss Viola said, her voice low and husky, staring deep into his eyes, "... people will think we are pursuing a courtship. Is that not shocking, your Grace?"

Ewan bit the inside of his cheek. There were any number of places they could have gone. He didn't believe that Lucas was in danger, of course, not with Emily and Hope to take care of him. But he was starting to feel that he couldn't stay where he was for a moment longer.

Not a single second.

He twisted in his seat, looking down at Miss Viola.

"Very shocking, I agree. We should be careful not to dance together twice, then. Perhaps dancing together even once would be risky. Don't you agree, Miss Viola?"

She blinked, taken aback, and glanced over to her mother for help. Ewan got to his feet, dusting stray cake crumbs from his suit.

"If you'll excuse me," he said shortly, addressing them all, "I see that Lucas and his nursemaid have gone off, along with Miss Barlow, no doubt. I shall go see if I can find them."

"Wait, I'll..." Miss Viola began, trying in vain to disentangle herself from her own dress.

Ewan didn't wait for her to get to her feet. He set off down the slope as fast as he could, not daring to wait even a second more.

Chapter Twenty-Three

It was a relief to leave that lopsided picnic blanket and their unfriendly neighbours behind. Hope was sick and tired of being so studiously ignored, and when Lucas asked if they could 'explore' she agreed immediately.

They walked towards a strip of woodland at a leisurely pace, with Lucas darting forward and back and all around them, picking up various items of interest and bringing his treasures back to his guardians to hold.

"I wish I hadn't come." Hope said levelly, when Lucas was at a safe distance. "I don't know what I thought would have happened."

"If you have an unexpected holiday day, it's always best to take yourself off." Emily said with a shrug. "But Lucas badly wanted you to come. He would have been so disappointed if you hadn't been here."

Hope bit her lip. She couldn't – wouldn't – admit to the truth. She wanted Ewan to want her to come. When he had asked for her to accompany them on their outing, she'd believed for a moment that he wanted her there. It had been a wonderful feeling. Swept off her feet, not thinking, Hope had agreed to come when she should have offered a polite deferral. Ewan's real feelings were fairly clear. He was sitting on the picnic blanket with his mother and her illustrious guests, making small talk with the flirtatious Miss Viola, while Hope felt like a prize fool.

Well, it was too late now. She might as well try and make the best of it.

Lucas came dashing back to them, holding aloft a small pebble that seemed to be vaguely shaped like a cat. He gave the pebble to Hope with a beaming smile and darted off to find another treasure.

Hope inspected the pebble, smiling to herself. "I'd give anything to be so carefree."

Emily chuckled, watching Lucas run in ever-growing circles. "I'd love to have that sort of energy."

Hope opened her mouth to say something else, some light-hearted comment, but a voice from behind stopped her dead in her tracks.

"Hope? Hope Barlow?"

Her blood ran cold in her veins. Emily glanced anxiously up at her, no doubt noticing the way Hope's colour drained from her face. She turned slowly, knowing exactly what – or rather, who – she would see behind her.

Lord Pembroke stood there, wearing a very fine walking suit, a pearl-handled cane clutched idly in one kid-gloved hand. He hadn't changed a bit.

"Auric." Hope gasped, more a reflexive thing than a conscious word. She caught herself, swallowing hard. "I mean, Lord Pembroke. What are you doing here?"

"What am I doing here, in Hyde Park? What do you think? I'm walking, you little fool."

She flinched at his tone. This was clearly not going to be a happy reunion. Not that Hope had expected it to be.

"I don't think you ought to speak to her like that, your lordship." Emily spoke up, her voice steady and cold. "It isn't proper for a gentleman."

Hope reached out and took Emily's hand, giving it a warning squeeze. Auric spared Emily a quick, disdainful glance.

"Gentlemanlike behaviour is only necessary when dealing with other gentlemen, or ladies. This young woman is certainly not the latter."

"Now, see here..." Emily began, taking a step forward, but Hope held her hand tightly, pulling her back.

"Emily, will you go and watch Lucas?" she asked desperately. "I don't want him to wander off."

Emily frowned. "I don't want to leave you alone with this man."

"I shall be fine. He's... an old friend, in a way. Go on, Emily, I don't want Lucas to get too far ahead."

She wavered, glancing over her shoulder at Lucas – who was indeed disappearing into the distance – and sagged a little.

"Fine. Very well. But I'll be within shouting distance."

Sparing a poisonous look for Auric, Emily strode across the grass towards the little boy, leaving Hope and Auric alone.

She eyed him closely for a moment. He really hadn't changed. It was strange to think that she'd once thought Auric the most handsome man in London – if not the whole of England, Scotland, Ireland, and Wales – and now his features seemed... well, indifferent. She could find no beauty in the curls of his hair, carefully styled over his forehead, or in his well-chiseled features.

Did I love him? She thought to herself. I'm not entirely sure. But I liked him, that was for sure. I liked him more than I dared admit even to myself.

Then Auric spoke, abruptly, shattering her musings.

"I'm surprised that you have the gall to show yourself here, after everything that happened."

Hope flinched. "I beg your pardon?"

He sneered, his handsome face crinkling up into something unpleasant.

"I think you heard me perfectly well. I heard that you went into hiding after you humiliated me so publicly, and I am somewhat shocked to see you out in so well-known a place as Hyde Park."

Hope was taken aback, needing a few minutes to respond.

"I humiliated you? I humiliated you? That's not at all how it happened!"

"Oh, my goodness, are we to go through this again? Have you no shame?"

"You broke off our engagement." Hope replied, careful to lower her voice. Nobody was nearby, but sound could travel shockingly well in an open space like this, and she didn't wish to risk being overheard. "You jilted me, Auric. Oh, I beg your pardon, Lord Pembroke."

"Don't be pert with me, little miss. I naturally ended the engagement when I found out that your wretched father lied about your dowry. What was I meant to do?"

Hope bit her lip, squeezing her eyes closed in an attempt to get back some of her composure.

She remembered her first and only Season, the way she'd skipped through the glitter and glow of countless balls, soirees, and parties. It had been wonderful in a bright, dizzying sort of way, something so wonderful and fairy-like that she was scarcely able to believe it was there.

With the solid surety of her dowry behind her, Hope knew that she was on a level footing with even the most beautiful ladies of the Season and was a fit prize for many of the eligible men.

When Auric first asked her to dance, her heart had started pounding madly, hopefully, eagerly.

It had all progressed easily from there. Auric called on her, leaving flowers and his calling card. He took her out to promenade in the Park, and they danced together at balls. Three dances for an engaged couple, two to demonstrate interest. They had danced many more than three dances on one occasion, Hope remembered. They'd danced together all night, laughing and dizzy from high spirits and good champagne.

And then Hope had discovered that her respectable dowry was nothing more than an illusion, and in fact she had not one penny to her name. Auric had learned it, too, and made his decision about their future very quickly.

That is, they would not have a future. Not together, at any rate.

It was barely consoling to know that Auric was not married and had not had an engagement or even an understanding with a lady since then. Hope didn't attribute that to any lingering feelings of love. No, it was more likely to be his own sour outlook and wariness.

"I am sorry that you were disappointed." She said aloud, aware that he was still glaring balefully at her, waiting for some reply. "I never meant for you to be hurt. But you chose to end our engagement. You chose that. I am not sure you can blame me for that."

Auric's eyes flashed, and she knew she'd made a mistake. He took a threatening step towards her, clutching his pearl-handled cane.

"See here, you little wretch. I had finally made a decision on my marriage, and all was to be well. Then I learn that you're the spawn of a debtor, some pathetic old gambler. How could I possibly attach our futures together?"

"That was your decision." Hope replied, pleased as how calm and level her voice was. "And I have learned to live with that. Since it was your decision, I'm sure you, too, can learn to live with it."

Auric's face went red with anger, and he took another step towards her. This time, Hope backed away. She realized with a sinking feeling that while they were in a very public park, there wasn't really anyone around.

"You embarrassed me in front of all of Society." He hissed. "Everyone knew I was engaged to you. Me, a viscount, a fine, upstanding man, one who could have married anyone I liked. Your father, on the other hand, was carted off to debtor's prison – shameful for anyone, let alone a member of the nobility."

Hope's temper flared. "And you think I wasn't suffering? I lost everything! I have nothing! Here I am, working as a... as a governess, when once I'd thought to be a viscountess. I'm not prepared for this life, and it is not easy for anyone."

Auric blinked in surprise, and Hope realized that she'd made a mistake.

"A governess?" he echoed, and Hope cursed herself for a fool. She wasn't sure what Auric had thought about her being here in Hyde Park after so long an absence. Perhaps he thought that she'd somehow regained the semblance of a position in Society. Perhaps he thought she had a more respectable position, like a companion.

Perhaps – and this was more likely – he simply hadn't thought at all.

Either way, the first tendrils of a nasty smile started to curl across his face.

"A governess?" he repeated, shaking his head. "My, my. That is shocking, don't you think? I am now congratulating myself on my lucky escape. Any woman who could lower herself to be a governess would certainly never make an appropriate viscountess. You might as well be a maid."

"How dare you?" Hope hissed. "You spoiled, smug, insufferable man. I see now that it was me who had the lucky escape. I cannot fathom what my life would be like now if I had married you. I had rather be a maid."

Auric jerked back at this, comically shocked.

"How dare I? How dare you, you little wretch! Now, see here, I'm not about to take such impertinence from a servant. You always did think you were better than me, didn't you?"

"I think our conversation is at an end." Hope said shortly, not sure why she'd stood there and listened to his nonsense for so long. She turned to leave, but Auric's hand shot out and grabbed her wrist in a vice-like grip.

Hope stared at him, waiting for him to release her. His grip only got tighter.

"Let go of me." She said, vainly trying to tug her arm away.

"You're no lady." Auric spat. "You were only ever the semblance of one. In fact..."

"I think you ought to let the lady go." Came a familiar, deep voice somewhere behind Auric's shoulder.

Auric flinched, letting go of Hope's wrist automatically. She whipped back her hand, cradling her bruised wrist to her chest.

Ewan stood behind Auric, a bland, impassive smile on his face. He was taller than Auric by at least half a head, despite the low heels on Auric's well-polished boots.

Auric blinked up at him, taking a moment to collect his thoughts.

"This is none of your concern, sir." He said shortly. "This vulgar woman and I were merely having a conversation. I'd thank you to mind your own business, please."

Ewan did not flinch. "This vulgar woman, as you so rudely describe her, is a member of my household, and I cannot and will not stand to see her bandied about in this way."

"Bandied about?" Auric spluttered. "How dare you, sir?"

"I saw you lay hands on her, in fact. Is that not so, Miss Barlow?"

Hope gave a brief nod, glancing down at her wrist. There were red marks where Auric's fingers had dug into her skin. There would be bruises later, she thought.

Auric's face had turned an interesting shade of red.

"Your household? You mean to say she is your governess?"

"She has the charge of my child, yes." Ewan said agreeably. "My only child. As such, she is a remarkably valuable part of my household. I must insist that you offer her an apology, sir."

Auric blanched. "An apology? To this harpy? I think not."

"I think you will, sir." Ewan said, his voice dropping low and ominous. He took a few steps forward, looming over Auric until the smaller man shuffled back nervously. "My good man, if you do not want to make an enemy of the Duke of Darenwood, you will offer your apologies at once and make yourself scarce. After that, you will take care that this young lady does not see your face again, which no doubt will not be a great loss to her. I am a formidable opponent, sir, with a remarkably long memory and a propensity for holding grudges. Is that clear?"

Auric's eyes widened in recognition. It seemed that while he hadn't been formally introduced to the Duke, he knew him by sight and reputation. He backed away faster, mumbling something that sounded like 'beg your pardon', vaguely aimed at Hope.

Then he turned tail and fled, heels slipping on the grass, nearly upending himself. Hope and Ewan watched him go.

She was suddenly aware of how shaky her knees had become.

I need to sit down, Hope thought tiredly.

"Now." Ewan said, before she could say a word. "Are you going to tell me what that was all about?"

Chapter Twenty-Four

Ewan took a few deep breaths, letting the anger settle down. He wanted nothing more than to go running after the disappearing man and give him a good kicking.

That wouldn't at all be appropriate, of course. He glanced over to where Emily and Lucas were playing a game of catch with a pinecone, reassuring himself that they were safe and comfortable, and then turned his attention back to Hope.

She was pale and preoccupied, and looked almost a little ill.

"I'd like to sit down." She said quietly.

"Of course." Ewan offered her his arm, which she took – much to his surprise – and he escorted her over to the only bench within sight.

The bench was barely large enough for two people to sit side by side. It was positioned at the edge of the woodland, with shrubs and trees clustering close around the bench, as if trying to swallow it up into the forest itself.

Hope sat down with a graceless thump. Ewan hesitated for a moment, not wanting to squeeze himself in beside her. But then, his alternative was to loom over her, which wasn't any more pleasant. Sighing, he fitted himself into the small remaining space, and waited for Hope to speak.

For a few moments, there was nothing but quiet.

Well, not exactly quiet. The birds were singing joyfully, and insects chirped in the woodland behind them. The wind shook the foliage ever so gently, so that a gentle rustling sound curled around them like mist. In the distance, he could hear Lucas' voice, laughing and chattering, and Emily's chuckles.

Miraculously, he couldn't hear Lady Harriet and Miss Viola, although he could see them silhouetted under the oak tree.

I like this, Ewan thought, with surprise. Sitting quietly here with Hope. This is... this is pleasant. Excepting that awful man that we just ran into, of course.

"He is my fiancé." Hope said, unexpectedly. "That is, he was my fiancé. His name is Auric, and he is the Viscount of Pembroke."

Ewan flinched, sucking in a breath. "I... I see. I didn't know that you were ever engaged."

Hope shrugged listlessly. "I only had one London Season before Papa's debts swallowed us up. I got engaged to Auric then. He broke things off when he found out that I had no dowry, and not a penny to my name."

"What an absolute scoundrel." Ewan said, with feeling.

Hope bit her lip, not meeting his eye. "I thought so once, but really, can I blame him? It wasn't simply going to be a case of marrying me without any money. He would be expected to help Papa get out of debtor's jail, and maybe pay off some of our creditors. It wouldn't be fair to him."

"Why would you ask a woman to marry you if you didn't intend to help them through all of their troubles?" Ewan muttered. "In sickness and in health, in poverty and riches. He ought to have stayed with you, if he truly loved you. Did... did you love him?"

He found himself holding his breath, waiting for her answer. Hope didn't reply for the longest time. Then she shrugged again.

"I thought I did. Now I'm not so sure. I liked him, at least. I wanted to marry him, and not just because he was a viscount. The thing is, when he discovered that I had no dowry, we were to be married in only a few days."

That changed the situation entirely. Ewan was glad he couldn't see the disappearing figure of Lord Pembroke anymore, as he would have been tempted to break the man's own walking stick over his head.

"He's a villain."

Hope sighed. "I thought so at the time. Papa had already paid for most of the wedding. I don't know how, since we had no money. I except he just sunk himself deeper into debt, hoping that Auric, as his son-in-law, would get him out of it again. I had no idea that my dowry was gone, of course. It was gone before it even began my Season."

Ewan frowned at this. He didn't feel sympathy for Auric – quite the reverse – but he couldn't blame the man for not wanting to have a sponging father-in-law. He glanced down at Hope, staring pensively off into the distance, and felt a wave of affection so strong he was glad he was already sitting down.

How could that man have not wanted to help her?

"Your father ought not to have put you in that position. It was unfair of him."

Hope pursed her lips, lost in thought. "My father was not a particularly good man, but neither was he a bad one."

Ewan searched his memory for any remnants of Hope's father. He could remember her mother well enough, a kindly, pleasant woman, but not her father.

"What was he like?"

Hope glanced up at him, a flash of surprise on her face, but it was quickly wiped away.

"My father was a kind man." She said firmly. "He loved me, and he loved my mother. When she... when she fell ill, he could not cope. He started drinking more frequently. He was never an angry or unpleasant man when he was in his cups, only... only foolish. He would come home, having lost his purse, and lie on the sofa in my mother's parlour and weep. He missed her so much. At the time, I didn't understand any of it, but I think that he drank to excess and gambled to deal with the pain of losing her. Not the wisest idea, but grief is a strange and powerful thing."

Ewan swallowed hard. He could agree to that. Caroline still lingered in the back of his memory, a bittersweet part of himself that would never really go away.

Lately, the pain had been easier to manage, though. Was that his imagination?

Hope gave a sigh, closing her eyes. "Papa told me that I had no dowry a week before the wedding. It didn't take me long to realize that I should go immediately to Auric and tell him the truth. So, I lost everything all at once. Auric, my father, my home, my position in Society, any respect anyone might have had for me. Everything was gone in one fell swoop. It seemed to happen so quickly. And I, like a fool, never even considered that Auric would end the engagement when I told him the truth. Papa told me not to tell him about the missing dowry until we were married, but I said that I couldn't keep a secret from him like that. I'm still glad that I was truthful, but I know now that Papa was banking on my marriage with Auric to save himself and me. He was taken to debtor's prison only a few months afterwards."

Ewan swallowed back a lump in his throat. He could only imagine how awful those months must have been for Hope. Reeling from the loss of the man she loved, trying to adjust to their new penniless state, Hope would then have had to say goodbye to her father, her home, her life. It must have been gut-wrenching.

"I'm sorry." He said at last. It felt like a silly thing to say, nowhere near powerful enough for the tragedies his old friend had just unfolded. "I had no idea."

She shrugged lightly, smiling. "Most people had no idea. We were a scandal for a while, of course. Auric and I, as well as Papa and me. People talked about us, gossiped, and then quickly forgot. And now, here I am. I've managed, you see. I came through it all. But I wish I hadn't seen Auric again today."

Ewan didn't realize what he was doing until he laid his hand over Hope's. She sucked in a breath, but didn't move her hand away.

"You have me." He said firmly. "We shall always be friends."

"Friends." She repeated, a soft smile on her face. "Yes, I suppose we will."

Abruptly, Hope got to her feet, shaking out her skirts.

"What is it?" Ewan asked, standing alongside her.

Hope avoided his eye. "I should go and catch up with Master Lucas and Emily. You should go back to your guests. I'm sure Miss Viola is waiting for you."

Without another word, Hope hurried away towards Lucas and Emily, leaving Ewan standing alone, baffled.

Chapter Twenty-Five

Downstairs, everything was in an uproar. The ball was happening tonight, and all of the servants were flapping around, trying to get things ready.

"Spell, 'bouncing'." Hope said, reading from the list of spelling words for today. It was a nice, easy task to round out the day, but Lucas was barely concentrating. The chaos downstairs intrigued him, and he was thrilled at the prospect of a real party happening at his own home.

"Do you think there'll be lots of people coming today?" Lucas asked.

"You'll be in bed before the guests start to arrive." Hope said severely. "Now, spell 'bouncing'."

"B-O-U-N-C-I-N-G." Lucas intoned obediently. "Are you going to the party?"

Hope flinched at that. "No, I won't be going."

"Why not? You came with us to the picnic, and to the Tower."

"That was different."

"Why is it different?"

Hope bit down on a sharp retort. Lucas meant no harm, she knew that. He really couldn't fathom why Hope shouldn't join the fine ladies and gentlemen downstairs. When he was older, he would understand, but for now... now, she didn't particularly want to explain it to him. It was too raw and new.

"It just is. I'm not invited." Hope said lightly.

"We could ask Papa if..."

"Right, I think we can finish lessons for today. What do you think? An early finish, so you can go and watch the ballroom being made ready for tonight?"

As expected, this distracted Lucas entirely. He beamed, grinning widely.

"I should love that! Thank you, Miss Barlow!"

"Excellent. Now..." Hope faded off at a gentle knock at the door. "Who is it?"

A familiar, red-haired gentleman peered around the doorway. Hope recognized him as Mr Sixsmith, Ewan's valet. He was a good natured and pleasant man, and well-liked by everyone, including Hope.

"Sorry to interrupt." Mr Sixsmith said with a grimace. "Her Grace, the Dowager, wants to see you in her private parlour, Miss Barlow. As soon as possible, she said."

"Of course." Hope said, trying to soothe her fluttering nerves. "We have just finished lessons. I didn't realise you were tasked with running messages, Mr Sixsmith."

He rolled his eyes. "Everything's in chaos over the party tonight. I have to go and help his Grace dress in a moment. The guests will start coming in a couple of hours, so there were no footmen free to carry the message. I'd hurry, if I were you. Her Grace isn't in the best of humour."

When is she ever? Hope thought but wasn't foolish enough to say it.

"Of course." She said instead. "Master Lucas, go to the nursery and find Emily. She'll see to your supper."

"Yes, Miss Barlow." Lucas chirped, bouncing away. Mr Sixsmith had disappeared, leaving Hope to collect herself in private and prepare to visit the Dowager.

Whatever the summons was, it couldn't be good. Hope guessed that the Dowager had chosen her moment carefully, so Ewan would not accompany her.

After the meeting with Auric yesterday, the four of them had returned to the picnic spot to be greeted with stony, angry faces. The Dowager reserved a particularly furious glare for Hope, and it was apparent that they were to be blamed for Ewan following them and therefore abandoning Miss Viola.

The day was ruined after that. Miss Viola was sulking, and Ewan made no move to talk to her in any case. Lady Harriet was ominously quiet, and neither Emily nor Hope dared break the silence. The Dowager chattered incessantly, obviously uncomfortable with the silence, until she had the bright idea of pretending to feel a spot of rain and insisting they all bundle back up in the carriages and go home.

Was this meeting about that? Hope couldn't say. She hoped not.

She had replayed the events of yesterday over and over in her head. Auric's harsh words, Ewan's heroic rescue.

Friends, he'd said. We shall always be friends.

That was a polite thing to say. A kind thing to say to an old friend that one pitied.

Hope hated pity. It was usually kindly meant, but the feel of it was like a thousand insects crawling on her skin, unbearable and cloying. She couldn't escape pity, it seemed, not even from Ewan.

He did not see her as an equal, and never would. She needed to accept that, the sooner the better.

Hope arrived in front of the Dowager's door and composed herself. She knocked, and immediately received the call to enter.

This time, there was no false smile or forced friendliness. The Dowager was writing diligently at her writing desk and did not look up at Hope when she entered. She gestured briefly for Hope to approach her desk, and continued writing.

Hope shifted from foot to foot, waiting nervously for the Dowager to speak. When she finally finished her letter, the Dowager looked up at her at last.

"Well, Miss Barlow." She said curtly, "You have a knack for making yourself noticed, do you not?"

Hope swallowed. "I don't know what you mean, your Grace."

"I think you do know what I mean. I'm sure my displeasure was quite clear at you dragging the Duke away from his guests yesterday. It was entirely inappropriate."

"I did not make him leave his guests, your Grace."

"Quiet!" the Dowager barked. "I won't stand for this insolence. Your duties here are to make the Duke's life easier and take care of Master Lucas. All I have seen so far seems to indicate you are taking up more of his time. This is not proper, Miss Barlow, do you understand me?"

Hope pressed her lips together, swallowing down the sense of anger and injustice.

"Yes, your Grace."

"Good." The Dowager seemed somewhat mollified. "Now, I have a few more words to say to you regarding tonight. First of all, you are not to make an appearance at the ball. Master Lucas will of course be coming down before bed – everyone will want to see him. But he will be attended by Emily and Miss Viola, not you. Is that understood?"

"Yes, your Grace."

There was a pause after that. The Dowager eyed her suspiciously.

"I am not sure I like your attitude, Miss Barlow. You seem to have an independent way about you. You do not like to be dictated to."

Does anyone? Hope thought but was wise enough to stay quiet.

"You may still see yourself as a lady." The Dowager continued brusquely. "As a person worthy of notice and respect. You are not. You are a governess, and if you cannot adjust to your new position in Society, you may not remain under our roof. This old friendship with my son is a very bad thing, and I suspect you have done great damage to yourself by claiming it. A governess is not friends with a duke. You have only shamed yourself by being so bold as to own up to such a thing. As to his Grace, my son, he is a good-natured man who is naturally inclined to kindness and pity. You are not to take further advantage of this is that understood?"

Hope clenched her hands into fists, hiding them in the folds of her skirts.

"I do not understand, your Grace." She said smoothly.

"Impertinence again! I mean that you are not to converse with his Grace unless it is absolutely necessary. Any matters regarding Master Lucas are to come to me first. In fact, I cannot see any reason why you would need to address his Grace at all. If he speaks to you, I suppose you must answer. However, I have reason to believe that his Grace's state will change very soon, and you will find that he no longer has the slightest interest in you."

Hope breathed in deeply through her nose. "His Grace's state?"

The Dowager narrowed her eyes. "I'll indulge your curiosity this once, because I think it will do you good to understand your true place in all of this. His Grace is about to become engaged."

Hope's breath caught in her throat. "Engaged?" she echoed.

The Dowager grinned. "Yes, engaged. There go all your clever, scheming plans, my girl. If you thought to entrap him by leaning on your old friendship, you are mistaken. My son may be a kind man, but not a foolish one. He realizes the value of good breeding and a fine dowry. Miss Viola will make a fine duchess."

He was marrying her, then. Hope swallowed hard, misery

welling up in her throat. It was all over. She'd thought... she'd been so sure... that Ewan felt something for her. She'd never imagine that he would stoop to marry a nasty, spoiled little impertinent child like Miss Viola.

I was wrong about him, she thought dizzily. He has changed.

The Dowager allowed herself a small, self-satisfied smile.

"As I said before," she said briskly, "You're to confine yourself to your rooms while the guests are here. That is all."

Hope bobbed a half-hearted curtsey and left. The Dowager had already turned back to her writing desk, and her pen had resumed its scritch-scratching before she had even reached the doorway.

***

Sounds of laughter wafted in through Hope's open window from the driveway below. Her room overlooked the courtyard and front gardens, and light from the countless candles and outdoor braziers lit up the window with a buttery glow, stronger than Hope's single, guttering candle.

She swallowed down a pang of misery. It was all over. Ewan was marrying Miss Viola. She couldn't imagine what his mother had said to convince him, but perhaps now that Caroline was dead, he didn't much mind who he married.

Pressing her hands against her ears, Hope tried in vain to drown out the sound of music and happiness from below. She imagined the ballroom filling up, full of light and cheer. She could almost taste the sweetmeats and crisp, fresh champagne. Her own dinner had not yet arrived, probably because the poor cooks in the kitchen were run off their feet. Her stomach rumbled, and Hope curled herself into a ball, willing herself not to cry.

She did not succeed.

Chapter Twenty-Six

Sixsmith considered himself the best valet in London, and he was probably right. He had offers almost every year from various noblemen, all keen to find out what the Duke paid him so that they could offer more.

They were fools, though. It wasn't about the money. Of course, the Duke did pay him remarkably well, but there were other perks to his position, too. Firstly, the Duke didn't insist on Sixsmith powdering his shockingly red hair, as other households might, and he allowed his valet a great amount of freedom.

More to the point, Sixsmith liked the Duke. He was pleasant to be around, friendly, and unaffected. It helped that he was tall, well-built, and handsome, which made him easy to dress well. A valet was only as good as he could make his master look.

For the ball tonight, Sixsmith had selected a deep green velvet suit. Perhaps not the most appropriate suit for a formal ball but flaunting the rules of fashion ever so slightly was, ironically, all the rage. He'd tied the Duke's cravat in a simple style – his Grace hated frothy lace and complex ruffles under his chin – and pinned an emerald cravat pin in the centre.

All told, he looked marvellous. And Sixsmith was very pleased with his own efforts. He gave the Duke's velvet-clad shoulders one last brush for luck, then stepped back demurely.

The Duke inspected himself with a smile.

"Thank you, Sixsmith. Excellent work, as always. You know, I always say that the only reason people even believe I'm a duke is because you dress me up like one."

Sixsmith allowed himself a small, pleased smile.

"Thank you, your Grace."

"Well, you might as well take the rest of the evening off. Don't bother waiting for me, I'll probably be late. This wretched ball won't finish early."

Sixsmith paused, hesitating. There was a tone of bitterness in his master's voice, one that wasn't often there.

"Your Grace? Is everything alright?"

The Duke paused, closing his eyes momentarily. "I'm just... just not looking forward to tonight, that's all."

"That's a pity, your Grace."

"Isn't it."

Sixsmith hovered near the door, just in case the Duke needed anything else. The man inspected himself in the mirror for a while, then spoke again.

"Have you met Miss Barlow, Sixsmith? The new governess?"

Why the change of subject? Sixsmith kept his expression smooth.

"Yes, your Grace, I have."

"Do you like her?"

He blinked. What was that supposed to mean?

"I like her very much, your Grace. She's a clever and hardworking young woman, and very pleasant to be around. Everyone likes her, I believe."

He saw the Duke give his reflection the tiniest of smiles.

"My son loves her. When I went to see him earlier, he said that he loves Miss Barlow, and wants her to stay forever."

"She is a remarkably good governess." Sixsmith said tactfully, not entirely sure where this conversation was going. There was a rumour below stairs that the Duke and Miss Barlow had once been friends when they were children. Naturally, gossip flew about, but not too much. The housekeeper and butler wouldn't allow it.

Still, it made one think, didn't it?

At least, it made Sixsmith think. He knew his master well, and it was clear that the Duke hadn't quite been himself since Miss Barlow arrived.

Could it be...?

No, Sixsmith scolded himself firmly. Enough of that.

"I do hope she is here to stay." He said lightly. "If I may be so bold, switching governesses so often cannot be good for Master Lucas."

"No, I agree." The Duke said firmly. "I told Lucas as such. I told him that Miss Barlow is here to stay, and that's the end of it. My mother is not fond of her, though."

He was speaking almost to himself at the moment, and Sixsmith wasn't sure whether to take his leave or not.

The Duke answered that question for him, shooting him a wry smile.

"Look at me, rattling on when you probably want to enjoy

your evening. Go on, off you go. Feel free to borrow a book from the library, if you fancy."

Sixsmith gave a bow.

"Thank you, your Grace." He paused at the door, glancing back over his shoulder. "For what it's worth, your Grace, I think that Miss Barlow is one of the finest women I have ever met."

The Duke was still staring, unseeingly, at his own reflection. He swallowed hard.

"I think you're right, Sixsmith."

***

"What is it, Harriet?" Margaret hissed, following her companion into the library. The room was dark, lit only by a few old candles. They wouldn't be using this room to entertain their guests, so it was shrouded and silent. The heavy velvet curtains, covering long, comfortable window seats, had been pulled across.

"I needed to be sure we wouldn't be overheard." Lady Harriet replied tartly. "Your son is not going to offer for my Viola."

Margaret pressed her lips together. "He will. I'm sure he will."

"Oh, and why are you so sure? Margaret, let me be plain. Your son has shown not the slightest interest in my girl since we've arrived. He's more taken with that wretched governess than anything else."

"The governess won't be at the ball."

"What does that matter?" Lady Harriet sighed impatiently, her myriad of tiny curls bouncing. Both women were ready for a grand ball. Lady Harriet wore a pale purple gown with too many ruffles, and her hair was a mass of tiny curls, twists, and ribbons. It must have taken hours to achieve, and the effect was not really worth it.

Margaret, on the other hand, had chosen a deep grey gown, cut from good silk, with white and black lace. It was a simpler affair, but fine enough for a ball. No doubt Miss Viola would be a real vision.

With a sinking feeling, Margaret realized that it would not matter. Ewan was not going to propose to Viola. They had wasted their time, because at the end of the day, he was drawn to that governess. Perhaps he would have the sense not to marry her, but it was bad enough.

"I won't allow myself to debase himself." Margaret hissed, a little taken aback at the hardness in her own voice. "We lifted ourselves from ignominy as a family, and I will not allow him to drag us back. This wretched girl is like a ball and chain attached to us. If we don't cut her loose, she'll drown us."

"A vivid image." Lady Harriet remarked. "But you can't command your son to marry at your will. He's of age, and he's a duke. He's beyond your reach."

Margaret bit her lip. "I know what is good for him. This is the right thing; I know it is. I have a plan, Harriet."

Lady Harriet blinked. "A plan? You? Forgive me for being so skeptical."

She rolled her eyes. "It's... it's a rather shocking plan."

"Don't tease me, Margaret. Tell me what it is."

Margaret drew in a deep breath, closing her eyes.

"If Viola is compromised by Ewan, he will have to marry her."

There was a long, tense silence.

"Explain." Lady Harriet said harshly.

"This is my plan. There is a small, secluded anteroom off the main ballroom. I shall send Ewan there on some pretext. There is a heavy curtain in that room, where you and I can peer inside. He won't see us. If we each bring along our ladies' maids, that will make for four witnesses. When Ewan goes to the anteroom, Viola must follow him."

"Unchaperoned?"

"That is the point. Of course nothing will happen, but then we will reveal ourselves, and you will demand to know what is happening to your daughter. You'll be shocked and angry, as it is deeply inappropriate. To avoid a scandal, Ewan will have no choice but to marry her. I shall insist upon it."

Lady Harriet considered this for a long moment. "That might work." She admitted. "Do you remember two seasons ago, when Lady Evangeline was caught standing very close to Mr Brummell on the terrace, with no chaperone in sight? They were married very hastily indeed."

Margaret nodded. "I recall. Well, that is my plan. It's a

shocking one, as I warned you, but…"

"I understand it." Lady Harriet said brusquely. "It's a risk, of course, but if we are careful… well, I hate to say it, but Viola's marriage prospects are not exactly brilliant. The Duke would be a fine match, and I don't much care how they get to the altar together. I'd say…" she broke off abruptly, ears pricking up. "Did you hear that?"

"Hear what?"

"I thought… thought I heard something." Lady Harriet glanced around, frowning. "Is someone else in here?"

"Of course not, not at this hour. It's dark. The library is shut up."

"I thought I heard a cough."

"Well, I heard nothing." Margaret said firmly. "What were you saying?"

Lady Harriet was quiet for a moment or two, seeming to listen. She gave herself a little shake, seeming to wake up from her reverie.

"It hardly matters. I think your plan is a good one. It's a last resort, at least. Are you sure you're willing to entrap your son into marriage?"

Margaret swallowed hard, straightening her spine.

"I am doing what I think is right for my son. He hopefully won't discover what I've done, and even if he did, I hope that he would understand. This is for the best. I am his mother, and I am Lucas' grandmother, and I know exactly what the best thing for him is, and that's that."

Lady Harriet eyed her for a long moment, then gave a short nod, seemingly satisfied.

"What we parents do for you children, eh?" she shook her head, sighing. "Come, let's go and get ready for this ball. We have a lot to talk about and a lot to plan."

Margaret nodded, feeling oddly relieved. They moved towards the door, with Lady Harriet casting one suspicious look back at the darkened library. They left together, closing the door behind them.

***

For a moment or two, the library was dead silent. After five or ten minutes or so, one of the heavy velvet curtains gave a twitch, pulling aside to reveal a comfortable, cushioned window seat. A man crouched on the seat, silhouetted against the buttery square of the window, lit from outside by flickering candlelight. The man leaned forward until his face came into view around the dusty velvet.

It was none other than the Duke's valet, his expression frozen in shock. He gave his head a tiny shake, as if unable to believe what he had just heard.

Sixsmith was curled up on the window seat, knees drawn up to his chest. His hand hovered over a book, now forgotten, dropped carelessly onto its pages and left there. His eyes were wide. He swallowed hard, his throat and mouth suddenly horribly dry.

It's like the stuff of a novel, he thought wryly, glancing down at the cover of the leather-bound tome he'd been reading. It is lucky beyond words that I always prefer the window seat.

It would never occur to the Dowager or Lady Harriet that a servant of all people would be in the library, reading.

He glanced carefully at the library door, making sure that the Dowager and Lady Harriet were not likely to make a reappearance anytime soon. The guests would be flocking in now, already crowding the halls. He might already be too late.

Chapter Twenty-Seven

The ballroom was packed with people. The air was full of chatter and laughter, clinking glasses and the faint strains of music. Ewan offered Margaret his arm, and she took it, somewhat hesitantly.

The servants had done a marvelous job. The ballroom looked like fairyland, with candles glittering everywhere, flowers on every flat surface, and beautiful music in the air. If only it wasn't for the people crowding into every corner, it would have been quite pleasant.

"Are you alright, Mother?" Ewan asked, peering down at her. "You seem preoccupied. Are you nervous about something?"

Margaret flinched. "Nervous? Nervous? Why would I be nervous?"

"What? Is something the matter? You aren't yourself."

Margaret gave a light, careless shrug. "I'm just worried about appearing in the scandal sheets for improper hosting."

"That's unlikely to happen."

She pursed her lips and said nothing. Ewan glanced down at his mother, a frown creasing his brow. Something was up. Was she really just nervous over the party? Or was she perhaps hoping that he would make an offer to Miss Viola tonight?

She would be disappointed if that was the case. Ewan was just thinking of ways to avoid Miss Viola and the wretched Lady Harriet when the two in question bore down on them, beaming.

"There you both are!" Lady Harriet chirped. "How handsome you look, your Grace. Now, when is the dancing going to begin? Viola is quite desperate to get started!"

Miss Viola simpered, tossing back her curls. She looked radiant today, wearing a rose-coloured silk gown that must have cost a fortune, and a hairstyle that must have taken hours to accomplish.

And yet she seemed uncomfortable, as if her fine clothes and hair were wearing her, instead of the other way around. It was strange.

Ewan flashed her a smile, tight-lipped and unfriendly as he could manage. When a moment of uncomfortable silence went by,

Miss Viola spoke up.

"Do not forget that you have promised me a dance, your Grace!" she said, smiling coyly.

"Oh, yes, you two must open the ball together!" Margaret exclaimed, clapping.

Ewan forced a smile. "Of course, of course."

He backed away, excusing himself before Miss Viola could entrap him into more conversation, and headed for the refreshment table.

It was going to be a long evening.

He snatched up a glass of champagne for himself and moved over to the mantelpiece to drink it in peace.

The night was moving along very well. He nodded and smiled at a few acquaintances, spotting a great many familiar faces.

And yet he didn't see the face he was looking for. Ewan drifted from face to face, his mood deepening.

"Why are you hiding over there, Ewan?" Margaret said, elbowing her way through the crowd towards him. "Why don't you go and talk to Miss Viola?"

Ewan bit his lip. "Miss Viola and I are not a match, Mother."

He'd expected her to be miserable, even angry at this, but Margaret only sighed and shook her head.

"As you like. I can't compel you to do anything, can I?"

"I suppose not. I take it Miss Barlow is not here tonight?"

Margaret glanced sharply at him. "Miss Barlow? The governess? Of course she is not here. Why, really. What a question to ask!"

Ewan drained his champagne, feeling the beginnings of a thumping headache at his temples.

"She was not always a governess, Mother. She and her family were once perfectly suitable association for us."

Margaret drew herself up, pressing her lips together in clear disapproval.

"Why must we go through this again, Ewan? I have no objection to Miss Barlow as a person, although she is too pert and forward for a governess. Time moves on, and so do we. It's not enough to be satisfied with what we once were. We are nobility now, and we must move in our own proper circle. Why can't you understand that?"

"Do you think we are too good for the Barlows of the world, now?"

"I certainly do." Margaret answered at once. "I know this is difficult for you, Ewan, but we need to embrace our place in life now. In the name of what is righteous, you have had enough time to come to terms with it now."

A flash of irritation went through him. Why could his mother never grasp this concept? Why could she not see how wonderful Hope was? Margaret seemed to believe that a comparison between Hope and Miss Viola would be bad for Hope, rather than the other way round.

"Evening, Ewan! Evening, your Grace. This is a spectacular party."

Robert appeared from nowhere, beaming. Margaret pursed her lips, glancing between them.

"Lord Ashbury." She said coolly. "I shall leave you gentlemen to converse. Mind you, Ewan, I except you to open the ball with Miss Viola, however. Do you understand? When the music begins in earnest, you must be on the dance floor."

Ewan set his teeth. "I know how to dance, Mother. I am aware of my obligations."

"See that you are! The poor girl has already written you down twice in her dance card."

The two men stayed silent while Margaret moved away.

"Twice, eh?" Robert remarked. "Dancing twice with the same lady denotes interest, does it not?"

"I am aware." Ewan muttered. "She probably wrote my name in her dance card herself. I will not dance with her twice."

There's only one woman I want to dance with, and she's not here.

"It seems like she's caught you, even so." Robert said, his voice carefully neutral. "I'm sure I warned you to have a care, my friend."

Ewan winced. "What am I to do? She's in my house."

"Your house." Robert said pointedly. "I have great respect for her Grace, the Dowager, but it is your house at the end of the day. I shouldn't let Miss Viola and her scheming mother stay much longer, if I were you."

Ewan bit his lip. "You're right, I just... I just don't know how to manage this business."

"Hm. Oh, before I forget, I have a message for you." Robert delved into his pocket and took out a neatly folded slip of paper. He handed it to Ewan, glancing around nervously as he did so.

Ewan was tempted to ask him who he thought might be eavesdropping, but his light words died on his lips when he saw the familiar, spiky handwriting.

"This is from my valet."

"Yes," Robert said, his voice low. "Good old Sixsmith waylaid me in the halls. He said he couldn't risk coming in here and finding you himself – it would be too obvious, a valet shouldering his way through the crowd – so he enlisted my help. He said that it was imperative that you should have that message as soon as possible. I've been looking for you since then, and here it is."

Ewan stared down at the folded slip of paper, a feeling of dread building in his stomach. Before he could open it, the first strains of waltz music started up. Couples began to hurry towards the dance floor, taking up their places.

"I'd better go." Ewan said reluctantly. "I'm to open the ball with Miss Viola."

Robert bit his lip. "I see. Good luck."

He drifted away, hands in his pockets – an action which would probably get his vouchers for Almack's withdrawn, if he were seen by the wrong person – leaving Ewan alone.

Stuffing the note, unread, into his pocket, Ewan headed towards the dance floor with a sigh.

Chapter Twenty-Eight

I don't want to be here. I don't want to be here.

The words swirled round and round Ewan's head while he danced, making his headache throb venomously.

Miss Viola was wearing a strongly scented perfume that was making him feel sick, and the light glinted off her jewelry and ornaments, shining painfully into his eyes until he wanted to squint when he looked at her.

She was talking to him about something, but Ewan was barely listening. This wasn't right, and he didn't want to be there.

I want Hope.

The thought solidified itself, and Ewan was struck with a feeling of yearning so powerful he almost wanted to double over. How could he have been so foolish? It was all so obvious.

He loved Hope.

It was impossible to tell where childish fondness had given way to a real, strong, adult emotion, but one thing was clear. Ewan could not recall a time in his past where Hope had not occupied a place in his mind and heart. He could not fathom a future where she did not occupy that same space.

Caroline would have hated Viola, Ewan thought with a wry smile. And she would have loved Hope. They'd have been friends, I'd bet my dukedom on it.

The whole thing seemed so laughably obvious that he wanted to chuckle to himself. Of course he was in love with her. There was no telling how Hope felt about him, of course. Ewan had never been good at judging those emotions from people, but he knew she had to be fond of him, at least.

He would tell her the truth. He would tell her exactly how he felt and wait to see what she said.

The dance came to an end, seeming to have lasted a hundred years, and Ewan bowed to his partner, heart suddenly light.

"We could dance another set, your Grace." Miss Viola said, a tinge of desperation in her voice.

"No, thank you." Ewan said abruptly, backing away. He almost bumped into Margaret. "Oh, Mother, I beg your pardon.

Excuse me."

"You aren't dancing again with Viola?"

"I am afraid not."

Margaret sighed but didn't push the issue. "Very well, I suppose I can't insist. Before you disappear into the crowds, could you do me a favour? I think I left one of my bracelets – the pearl one, the one that matches this necklace – in the little reading room in the corner. Could you find it for me? I'm terribly afraid that I've lost it. I'd ask a servant to fetch it, but they're all so busy."

Ewan bit his lip, looking down at his mother's calm, earnest face.

"Of course, Mother. I'll fetch it at once."

As he made his way to the anteroom, he hastily retrieved the missive from his pocket and perused its contents. The note proved to be of such a nature that it rendered him utterly dumbfounded, incapable of uttering a single word.

The reading room in the corner was a tiny little anteroom, furnished with a couple of bookshelves and a small armchair. It was separated from the main room by a heavy velvet curtain instead of a door.

The room was lit by a single candle, burning fiercely on a low table. With the curtain pulled across and only moonlight coming in through the small, round window, Ewan squinted in vain, trying to spot the glimmer of pearls.

Soft footsteps, muffled by the rug, sounded behind him, and there was the distinct sound of the curtain being pulled back across. Ewan turned to find Viola standing there, hands folded demurely before her.

He frowned. "Miss Viola, can I help you?"

"I just wanted to talk, your Grace."

"We had better talk in the ballroom. It's not proper to talk in such a secluded place."

He took a step forward, intending to return to the main room, but Viola did not budge. She stood between him and the doorway, so he would have to push her aside if he wanted to leave.

If he did that, she would most probably scream.

"I don't care about proper." Viola breathed. "I enjoyed our dance very much, your Grace. You intrigue me."

"Do I? It was not intentional." Ewan said shortly. "Miss Viola,

I must tell you for the second time that this is not proper. I know what you are trying to do, and it will not work."

Her gaze shot up at him then, and he saw a flare of dislike, hastily replaced by smooth coyness.

"I have no idea what you mean, your Grace. I am only telling you how I feel."

"No, I think you are telling me what your mother has told you to say. And I am telling you that I would like you to stop. I'm sure you'll marry a perfectly suitable man one day, if that is what you wish, but it isn't me. I'm sorry, Viola."

Confusion crossed her features, hastily smoothed away.

"Your Grace, your words are hurtful. I feel a connection between us, truly I do. Do you not feel it?"

She moved forward, hand stretched out to touch his chest. The anteroom wasn't large, and Ewan struggled to avoid her. If he knocked over a table or made a noise in there, they might be overheard, and then all would be lost.

"Meeting me in here could make me obliged to marry you, if it was discovered." Ewan said sharply.

"Would that be the worst thing in the world, your Grace?"

"Yes, because I am in love with another."

That stopped Miss Viola dead in her tracks. Her features clouded, suddenly spiteful.

"Not that plain little governess?"

Ewan stepped nimbly around her, a few feet nearer now to the exit.

Miss Viola seemed to recover her equilibrium and pressed on. "Well, it doesn't matter. We are here, your Grace, entirely unchaperoned, and..."

"Not entirely unchaperoned, you see." Ewan shot back, whisking back the curtain.

Hidden carefully in the folds of the curtain were Lady Harriet, Margaret, and two hapless-looking maids.

Lady Harriet blanched, glowering at her daughter.

"You were supposed to keep him from the curtain, you little ninny?"

Viola scowled. "I tried, but he was too fast."

"This is a clumsy and entirely inappropriate ploy." Ewan said sharply. "Lady Harriet, I might have believed this of you, but I thought my mother at least would have a little integrity."

Margaret had the grace to blush, cringing.

Lady Harriet was uncowed. She lifted her chin, meeting Ewan's eyes squarely.

"It matters not. I, your own mother, and these two maids have seen you and Miss Viola closeted away here, unchaperoned. It is highly improper. You, sir, have compromised my daughter, and in recompense you must marry her."

"That would be shocking indeed, if the whole scene had not been set up by you beforehand. I happen to know that you were here the whole time. So we were, in effect, chaperoned." Ewan shot back.

"What terrible lies! Why, I..."

"You were overheard." Ewan said simply, and Lady Harriet trailed off.

He reached into his pocket, pulling out a crumpled note.

"A gentleman of my household overheard you and my own mother plotting to set up this scene. The note was delivered to me before the dancing began by another gentleman who, I am quite certain, has also read it. If you choose to pursue this matter, madam, you will not win. You will be exposed as a vile schemer, and Miss Viola will be ruined even so. I will not marry your daughter, madam."

Lady Harriet, for once, was at a loss for words.

"Overheard." She hissed eventually. "I knew I heard something."

"Will you say anything about this?" Viola piped up anxiously, wringing her hands together. "I'll be ruined..."

"I certainly shall not, but perhaps bringing along two maids as witnesses was a mistake." Ewan pointedly turned his back on Viola, stepping back out into the main ballroom. He smiled sweetly at Lady Harriet. "I trust you and your daughter will be packed up and ready to leave within the hour. Get out of my house, Lady Harriet. If I were you, I would not return."

He turned and walked away without a backwards glance, even when he heard a soft thump that may or may not have been Lady Harriet fainting.

Chapter Twenty-Nine

The next day dawned bright and clear. The sun was just rising, and the last guests had taken their leave only a few hours before.

It seemed amazing to Ewan that despite everything that had gone on, the guests were still happy and cheerful, enjoying themselves and chattering merrily.

He hadn't slept at all that night. He didn't even feel tired.

An early morning mist was creeping along from the fields, swirling along the gravel driveway beneath his study window. It almost looked like the grounds were springing out of a white, foggy sea. It was picturesque, in a serious, ominous sort of way.

"You wanted to see me, Ewan?" Margaret said stiffly, appearing in the open doorway.

"Yes, Mother. Come in, sit down, please." Ewan turned back from the window, indicating the two armchairs by the fire. It seemed less harsh and formal than his desk.

Margaret was still wearing her somewhat bedraggled finery from last night. Her pearl bracelet, of course, had never been in the anteroom at all. In the harsh morning light, she looked tired and frail, the grey silk draining her of colour.

"I suppose you are angry with me." Margaret said shortly. She sat straight-backed on her seat; lips pursed together.

"I suppose you are." Ewan replied, settling himself opposite. "You look angry."

"I am angry with you. You shamed me before my friend. I should like you to apologise to Lady Harriet and to her poor daughter. Your accusations..."

"You have been trying to force me to marry Miss Viola since the hour she arrived. Didn't you, Mother? And you were piqued when I didn't obey."

Margaret scowled. "Well, I put a very fine option before you, Ewan. Miss Viola is a fine catch."

"I'm sure. But I did not want to marry her. I made that clear. You went behind my back, Mother."

Margaret had the grace to blush. She looked away, picking at a piece of lace on her sleeve.

"I had nothing to do with that business in the anteroom." She mumbled. A pitiful lie.

"Yes, you did. You were overheard. Why are you lying to me about it? Can you not see that I cannot trust you anymore?"

Margaret flinched at that. "It was an extreme thing to do, I see that now. I was just... well, I was just afraid."

"Afraid of what?"

She sighed. "Afraid that you would not marry Miss Viola."

"I made it clear that I would not. Mother, I'm not a child. You can't try and trap me into things like that. What if I hadn't been warned? I don't love Viola. I couldn't love her."

"Love is not..."

"Please don't tell me that love is not important to a happy marriage. I was married happily to Caroline. I know what it is to marry a woman I love, and who loves me. I know what it is to have respect, affection, and a genuine care for each other in a marriage. Caroline was not perfect, but she had many good qualities. She and I brought out the best in each other. Why would I settle for less if I chose to marry again?"

A long silence stretched out between them. Ewan had the sense that his mother had managed to justify her actions to herself, but now that they were done and she had been discovered, those justifications seemed hollow.

When it was obvious that she was not going to speak, he sighed.

"Come on, Mother. Tell me the truth. Why did you do this?"

Margaret swallowed hard. "I was afraid that you would marry that governess."

"Who I marry is my business. You deceived me. You deliberately lied to me, trying to entrap me in a situation where I would have no choice but to marry a woman I do not like and could not respect. You are my mother. How can you betray me like this?"

Tears welled up in Margaret's eyes.

"Because I know that if you marry again, I'll be cast off and forgotten about! You'll send me away, and you won't need me anymore. I knew that if you married a lady like Viola, I would continue to be important."

"You thought I would send you away?" Ewan said softly. "I would never have done that, no matter who I married. It's strange that you think that, because I can't imagine Miss Viola would be happy to share the role as mistress of a house."

Margaret flushed at that, and Ewan suspected she was starting to see the flaws in her plan.

"It was a mistake, I grant you, but my intentions were good." She said firmly, tilting up her chin.

Ewan looked away, eyeing the smoldering wreck of the fire.

"You weren't thinking of me, Mother. Please, don't pretend that you were. Don't you see that I now can't trust you anymore? I will always be afraid that you're going to try and trap me into marriage. You did all of these things without stopping to think that perhaps it was wrong. You were going to force me into marriage! Do you truly believe that you were justified?"

"I did what I thought was best!" Margaret snapped. "I have always done what I thought was best. This is all because of that governess. She is weighing you down. She is weighing us down. She is a reminder of what we once were, and if you do not cut her off soon…"

"I am not ashamed of what we once were, as you so nicely put it." Ewan said quietly. "I am sorry that you are ashamed. Hope is my friend and will always be my friend. You will always be my mother, but I can't trust you to live here with me anymore. How do I know you won't try again? What might you try to do to Lucas, believing that your intentions are good, and your judgement correct? You must leave my house, Mother."

There was a tense silence between them, stretching out for a full minute. Margaret's eyes were wide, tears drying on her cheeks.

"You are sending me away?" she whispered.

"I am not sending you anywhere. I don't control your life. You can go where you like, although I have arranged for you to travel back to the Dower House today. I won't keep you from Lucas, although you will have to content yourself with occasional visits. I will not let you live with my son and I anymore. I'm sorry."

Margaret gave a sobbing breath, clutching a damp handkerchief.

"How can you be so cruel? I am your mother! After everything I have done for you, you still refuse to oblige me? I insist that you undo all of this! This is not right! I will not allow my authority..."

"I am the Duke of Darenwood, Mother." Ewan said softly. "You have no authority here. I trusted you. I didn't just trust you with myself, but with my son. I know you won't believe it, but I do love you. I just can't allow you to stay, and you won't change my mind."

Margaret stumbled to her feet and charged out of the room, weeping loudly all the way.

Chapter Thirty

Hope craned her neck, watching the carriage rumble away down the drive. If gossip was to be believed, that carriage carried the Dowager Duchess, leaving for the countryside, never to return.

She would believe it when she saw it, of course.

She, Emily, and Lucas had holed up in the schoolroom, making a nest from blankets and cushions, reading picture books and eating a rather fine cake left over from last night.

Something had happened, Hope sensed it in the air, but everyone seemed rather reticent about what that something actually was.

A tap on the door woke her up from her reverie. Ewan peered around the door, and Hope's heart began to thump.

"I'm sorry to interrupt." He said apologetically. "Emily, could you take care of Lucas for a moment? I would like to speak to Miss Barlow for a moment."

Emily eyed Hope worriedly, but nodded obediently.

Hope slipped out of the schoolroom after Ewan, following him down the hallway.

"Do you mind if we take a walk outside?" Ewan asked over his shoulder. "I could do with stretching my legs, and it's a fine, fresh day."

"Of course, your Grace." Hope said lightly.

"Oh, another thing. We really need to put a stop to you calling me your Grace."

"I... I don't understand."

"I shall explain in a moment. Now, did you hear what happened last night?"

Hope blinked, confused. "Do you mean, the ball? It sounded very fine, but the Dowager instructed me to stay in my rooms, out of the way."

Ewan's expression hardened. "Yes, I can imagine she did. Well, to cut a long story short – and I can rely on your discretion, I know – Lady Harriet and my mother conspired to put me and Miss Viola together, so as to compromise us and force us to marry."

Hope stopped dead. "What?"

"Oh, I think you heard me. Wait till we get outside, and I'll tell you more."

Ewan led the way through the foyer, and out of the front door. Hope paused on the doorstep, closing her eyes and breathing in deeply. It had rained sometime during the night, and the air smelled fresh and green, of damp earth and flowers. A few tendrils of mist still clung to the edges of the fields, and there was a pleasant chill in the air.

She opened her eyes and saw that Ewan was standing on the gravel walkway, looking up at her with a strange look on his face.

"Walk with me?" he asked, tilting his head.

Hope smiled. "Of course, your Grace."

"I think you ought to call me Ewan. It's strange to have a childhood friend calling me that."

"I don't think her Grace, the Dowager, would be pleased with that." Hope said gently.

Ewan swallowed hard, looking away. "My mother has left my house. She is going to live in the countryside."

Hope glanced at him sharply. "Truly? Oh, I am sorry."

"Don't be sorry. She tried to trap me into a marriage. It's... it's a betrayal that I won't quickly recover from. My mother and I need a little time away from each other, I think."

They walked side by side for a few minutes in silence. Hope struggled to absorb this information. The Dowager was really gone, just like that.

"I take it that Lady Harriet and Miss Viola are gone, too?" she asked warily.

Ewan nodded. "I was lucky. My valet – I must give that man a raise, really – happened to overhear them, and sent word to me about what they planned, so I was prepared. But it could easily have worked out otherwise, and then I would be announcing my engagement to Miss Viola right now."

Hope winced. "I know it's not proper to say, but I don't like her very much."

"Neither do I. Neither does Lucas, in point of fact. I find that children are often a very good judge of character."

"I agree." Hope said eagerly. "They're so innocent and insightful, they see straight through lies and subterfuge. We can all learn a lot from the honesty of children."

Ewan smiled down at her, and this time Hope saw fondness

in his eyes.

"Can I be frank with you, Hope?"

"Of course, your Grace. That is… Ewan." Hope smiled to herself. It felt strange saying the name out loud, but also just right. "I've missed using that name, I think."

Ewan reached out, taking her hands in his. The contact sent tingles along Hope's skin, and she sucked in a breath, eyes wide.

"I am in love with you, Hope." Ewan said simply. "I don't think I can remember a time when I was not in love with you. I've always carried a part of you with me, ever since we were children. I know you and I have lived different lives, and I dare say we have a great deal to catch up on, but the fact is that you are another part of me. The better part, of course. I could never have married Miss Viola for a number of reasons, but one in particular stands out."

"She is insufferable?"

Ewan smiled at that. "She is not you, Hope Barlow."

Hope swallowed hard, not daring to let the happiness wash through her.

"Ewan, you should know that I really do have nothing. I told you that I have no dowry, and that is true. I haven't even had time to save up any of my wages. I have no money, no status, no place in Society. My father is still in debtor's prison. I have nothing. I am nobody."

"That's not true." Ewan said hotly. "You are Hope Barlow, you are not a nobody. And as to nothing – well, what would you call intellect, charm, beauty, and kindness? You are the most remarkable person I have ever met. Lucas adores you. The household loves you. You win the respect of everyone you meet. What's more, you have my heart, if you want it."

Hope had to smile at that, feeling as though her face might split in two.

"Then would it be appropriate to tell you that you have mine, too? I love you too, Ewan."

"That would be very appropriate." Ewan said, gathering her in his arms and pulling her close to him.

He kissed her, the warmth of his palms soaking through Hope's gown. She wound her arms around his neck, feeling the feathery-soft ends of his hair against her fingertips.

"Will you marry me, Hope Barlow?" Ewan murmured, when

they broke apart to breathe.

Hope had never understood the phrase 'feeling so happy one could burst', but it made sense now. She beamed up at him, wondering if it was all a dream after all.

If it is a dream, she thought, I had better not wake up.

"Of course I will marry you." She whispered. "I have dreamed of nothing else."

Ewan's face split into a smile. "We'll face a great deal of disapproval."

"It won't be anything that I'm not used to."

"In that case, we had better go and break the good news to Lucas. He'll be thrilled at the prospect of a new Mama, and even more thrilled to learn that his new Mama is you."

Epilogue

One Year Later

"Can I hold her?" Lucas asked eagerly.

"Of course you can." Hope said, beaming down at him. She gently transferred the tiny baby, swaddled in linens, into Lucas' waiting arms. Ewan sat behind him, ready to steady Lucas if need be.

The baby barely stirred, her tiny lips pursing as she slept. Lucas stared down at her with open adoration.

"She's so pretty." He said, his voice hushed. "I like the name Helen."

"It is a nice name, isn't it?" Ewan said, smoothing out a wisp of fair hair on the top of Baby Helen's head.

"Can I play with her?"

"Not yet, I'm afraid." Hope said, ruffling his hair. "Helen is a little bit too small to play just yet. But you can hold her, and talk to her, and help Emily tuck her up in her crib."

"Can I read to her? I think she'll be very impressed by how good my reading is now." Lucas asked seriously.

Hope suppressed a smile. "I'm sure she will. You certainly can."

Lucas beamed around at them. "I like having a little sister."

Ewan pressed a kiss to the top of his son's head, smiling at Hope.

"We like her very much, too."

"Shall I take her back to the nursery, your Graces?" Emily asked, hovering in the background.

"Yes, thank you, Emily." Hope replied.

"Can I come?" Lucas asked eagerly.

"Of course you can. Be gentle with your little sister, though."

Emily slipped away with baby Helen cradled in her arms, with Lucas skipping along behind her. That left Ewan and Hope alone in their drawing room.

"I'm exhausted already." Ewan murmured. He draped his arm over the back of the sofa, taking Hope's hand in his. Running his fingertip over the curve of her wedding ring, they exchanged tired smiles.

"I get the feeling parenthood is not going to get any easier." Hope observed.

Ewan winced. "I'm afraid not."

It had been over a full year since their marriage, with baby Helen being born only a day before their anniversary date. The wedding itself had been quiet and unobtrusive, but of course the scandal hit the gossip columns shortly afterwards. Between Lady Harriet and her daughter's impropriety and a duke marrying a governess, the scandal sheets didn't know what to focus on.

Hope always pitied Miss Viola, in a way. She didn't know how the story of what she and her mother had planned had leaked out, but it had, and Lady Harriet had immediately whisked her daughter away to the countryside. A handful of the ton refused to acknowledge Hope, but the rest did find her agreeable and pleasant. She had friends now, and that made the disapproval more bearable.

And, of course, she had Ewan. Hope flashed another smile at him, leaning forward for a kiss.

"If you'd told me a year and a half ago today that I would have married my oldest friend, a duke, I would not have believed you." She remarked.

He chuckled. "If you'd told me a year and a half ago today that I would be married again at all, I would not have believed you."

Hope squeezed his hand. "Lucas was asking questions about his mama today. I showed him her portrait, I hope that's alright?"

"Of course it is. Caroline will always have a place in my heart."

"Exactly. There's no need to forget her."

Ewan lifted a hand to cup Hope's cheek, his gaze soft and affectionate.

"What on earth did I do to deserve you, my darling Hope?"

"You were very lucky." She said, as seriously as she could manage. "Did you write to the Dowager about Helen?"

Ewan winced, and Hope saw real pain in his eyes.

"I did, but no reply yet. I am hoping she'll write back this time. She hasn't seen Lucas since she left."

Hope swallowed hard. This, she knew, was a sore point for

Ewan. He did love his mother, and Lucas was very fond of his grandmother. But Margaret was too proud, and simply would not give in. She wrote occasional letters, but the letters often carried accusations and excuses. She had never once apologized, not really.

She had not attended their wedding, even though she was invited. Hope often thought that if she had come, it would have done a great deal to patch up the relationship between her and her son.

But that was in the past. Hope had written letters to Margaret too, but she never received a response. Lucas had stopped asking after his grandmother altogether, and that broke Hope's heart.

"Should we invite her to stay with us? As an olive branch?" Hope suggested.

Ewan bit his lip. "I don't know. I told her all about Helen in my letter, and I want to wait and see what she has to say. Perhaps... perhaps this will be the thing that knits us back together. It's just difficult to know that she doesn't understand how badly she hurt me. If she'd had her way, I would have been tricked into a miserable marriage with Viola. I would have betrayed myself and let down Caroline, as well as sentencing Lucas to a miserable childhood. I would have lost you, my love."

Hope squeezed his hand reassuringly. "But you didn't lose me, did you? Regardless of whether Margaret decides to patch up our relationship or not, you must realise that you did the right thing."

He nodded slowly. "I know, I know. You're always so practical, and so sensible."

"Well, one of us has to be." Hope joked, getting to her feet. "Now, I'd better oversee preparations. My aunt and cousin should be here soon."

"Ah, excellent. I haven't seen Ruth and Agnes for a good few months."

Hope beamed at him. She had been nervous when introducing her Aunt Ruth and cousin Agnes to Ewan. What if they didn't like each other?

She needn't have worried. They got on tremendously well.

What was more, somebody else was coming up for a visit

alongside them, someone Hope hadn't seen for many years.

Somebody whose affairs had taken Ewan almost a year to extricate.

Ewan reached out and took her hand again.

"Your father is thrilled to be seeing you again after so long. You read his letters, remember." Ewan said softly. "Everything will be alright, I promise."

"I know, I know." Hope said, smiling nervously. She paused, tilting her head. "Is that a carriage coming up the drive?"

"It seems so." Ewan replied, craning to look out of the window. "Ah yes, here they are. They're early."

Hope gave a delighted shriek and went darting out into the courtyard. Ewan followed her, laughing as she jumped up and down like a child, waving wildly.

"My mad little governess." He murmured to himself, pressing a kiss to the top of her head. "How I do love you."

The End

Printed in Great Britain
by Amazon